The Shootout Solution

Also by Michael R. Underwood

The Ree Reyes Series
Geekomancy
Celebromancy
Attack the Geek
Hexomancy

The Younger Gods
Shield and Crocus

EPISODE 1

GENRENAUTS

The Shootout Solution

MICHAEL R. UNDERWOOD

A TOM DOHERTY ASSOCIATES BOOK

NEW YORK

THE SHOOTOUT SOLUTION

Copyright © 2015 by Michael R. Underwood

Cover art by Digital Vision Vectors/Getty Images

Edited by Lee Harris

A Tor.com Book

Published by Tom Doherty Associates, LLC

175 Fifth Avenue

New York, NY 10010

www.tor.com

Tor® is a registered trademark of Tom Doherty Associates, LLC.

ISBN 978-1-4668-9194-4 (e-book)
ISBN 978-0-7653-8532-1 (trade paperback)

First Edition: November 2015

To my dad, for bringing home countless
Louis L'Amour books on tape when I was a kid

The Shootout Solution

Prologue

Inciting Incident

MALLERY YORK PRESSED HER BACK against the outer wall of the saloon while bullets flew on Main Street. Her breath came fast as her hand fumbled, ripping the hem of her skirt and tying another bargain-basement tourniquet around her right arm. It'd keep the bleeding down, but she'd taken three hits, and addressing them all would transform her outfit from "Western" to "Jane of the Jungle."

The report of gunshots came around the corner, impacts sending splinters of wood flying in the dusty street. Mallery flinched at each one, every hit refreshing the sharp pain from only moments ago. She'd gotten lucky, in that "not all bullet wounds are created equal" kind of way. But no matter what, the mission had gone down the latrine and it was time to bug out.

Mallery dug into her petticoats for the polished chrome and Gonzo Glass phone. Doubling over to make herself a smaller target, she pressed the big red button, shielding the phone from view. Even with bullets flying, she kept to the concealment protocol, just as regs demanded.

The call picked up on the second ring.

"This is King. What's your status?"

"Floundering in a sea of gunfire and dust."

"Just hold on," King said. The voice of her boss and mentor was a life preserver. She grabbed it and held on for dear life.

"The showdown was a bloodbath. Our White Hats are down to the last man, and I saw him turn tail and run a minute ago. The bandits are going to finish off the wounded in a minute, and I need immediate evac."

Someone moved on the other end of the line, set to speakerphone. Probably Preeti rolling over to another station. "What happened?" King asked. "You said you had the posse assembled, they had their bonding scene around the card table and everything."

"Tell that to the three dead deputies in the street, boss. What's my ETA on an extraction?"

Low chatter between Preeti and King. Then, "Roman will be there in ten minutes. Can the story be salvaged?"

Mallery risked a look out into the street, concealing the phone beneath her sweat-and-dust-stained hair. The bandits were tying bags from the bank to their saddle-bags, but the gunfire had calmed down.

"Not today. We'll need to assemble another posse."

"Understood. Stay out of harm's way, and Roman will be at your location in fifteen."

Mallery winced. "I thought it was ten?"

"Dimensional disturbance. Preeti has plotted a new course, but it's going to delay the crossing."

"Well, I'll just hang out here and bleed some more, then. No big problem."

"Try to keep that to a minimum," King said.

"Aye aye, captain."

"Preeti will stay on the line with you until Roman arrives. Be careful, Mallery. King out."

"Careful isn't going to stop the bleeding," Mallery said, watching her skirt go red. Next time she came to Western-land, she was wearing the chaps. They were at least something resembling armor. Though they couldn't be turned into bandages nearly as easy. You give a little, you get a little.

"Roman is on his way. We've got your location locked, so just sit tight," Preeti said.

"You know, this is why I prefer Romance world. At least there I'd be having mortal-danger makeouts while under fire."

"I'll put in the request on your duty roster. More mortal-danger makeouts."

"I don't know about more, but I'll take it."

Preeti stayed on the line, trying to engage Mallery with small talk, keeping her bleeding friend focused when the world started to go black. Mallery leaned into the conversation, shutting her eyes and focusing on Preeti's story about spending all Saturday digging through the source text archives to find her favorite childhood storybook.

Mallery ducked her head out to check on the bandits. The Williamson gang had finished loading up and was riding for the hills with half of the town's silver. "When I get back, I am so kicking someone's ass."

Another impact hit mere feet from her head. She ducked and said through clenched teeth, "This is *not* how the story was supposed to end."

One

Everyone's a Critic. Even Drunks.
Especially Drunks.

LEAH TANG WAS DYING ON STAGE.

She knew she shouldn't expect too much from a college bar crowd, but this was beyond the pale.

Her *The Last Action Hero* bit? Interrupted every ten seconds by the table full of bros up front yelling for her to show some flesh.

Her breakdown of why the Star Wars prequels failed, from the lack of a scruffy-looking-Nerf-herder rogue figure to the bungling misuse of the Jedi Order? Nothing but heckling.

Even her story about the Epic Ice Fortress Snowball Wars from when she was in middle school fell flat, and that bit had killed before.

It sure didn't help that the drunk first-timer before her had gotten a hooting-and-hollering standing ovation with nothing more than five minutes of boob jokes.

He'd primed the audience so much that when she took the stage, one of the bros up front asked her to flash him. It was a testament to her professionalism that she didn't just dump her water on his head to start off her set.

In fact, so far the only person in the room who seemed at all interested in her routine was the intense black guy sitting on his own in the second row by the entrance. He hadn't taken his coat off even though the bros up front were sweating in the lights. This guy, this one appreciative audience member—he liked her genre commentary, so she'd be happy to oblige.

This guy had been at her last open night too, if she remembered right. So he was either digging her work, a creeper, or maybe both. Hopefully not both. That wouldn't bode well for her future fan base. "I'm huge with the 'overly intense and creepy' crowd!" Not so good.

Not that she had a fan base to begin with. The rest of the crowd—the townies at their regular tables and the drunk-ass students up front—the best they managed was polite disinterest.

Leah heard her father's voice in her head. "Oh, Leah, don't go to the coast and become a comedian. Make a responsible choice; stay here with your family and go to optometry school like your brother."

The bros up front catcalled again, asking for her number for the third time.

"Come down here, baby!" one said. "I'll make your fantasies come true."

Cal, the owner, had a very high bar for throwing out belligerent hecklers, so she was on her own. It was three strikes and you're out here at the Attic, and she was in the middle of Strike Three. So she might as well enjoy herself.

"Fantasy, eh?" Leah asked.

Perform for the audience you have, not the audience you want, she thought. She grabbed the available segue and ran with it, squaring off to the audience and zeroing in on the bros in the front row.

She affected a coquettish bedroom voice. "Let me tell you about my fantasy."

That got the bros' attention.

"My fantasy"—hooting and howling nearly drowned her out. She resumed, trying to shut them out. "Discovery. New races, new kingdoms, new magics. I loved that when I opened a fantasy book or found a new author, I knew I was in for a tour through someone's imagination."

The bros were crestfallen, their interest shorted out. But the guy in the coat leaned forward, elbows on the table, his drink sitting forgotten beside him.

"But as I grew up, I realized something that was incredibly rare in fantasy: people that looked like me.

"In most fantasies, an Asian girl like me only shows

up as a topless witch in need of rescue or killing, with snakes crawling over her boobs. And that is just not my scene.

"My fantasy is less about the whips and the PVC, more about self-actualization and hope. And you know what? That's just as sexy to me."

That got a chuckle out of one of the college guys up front. From the look of him, thickly muscled, wearing a tank top that read "No Fat Chicks," he was probably not laughing at the joke the way she meant him to be.

"In my fantasy, Asian girls like me can do anything we want. We can be fighters, wizards, and rogues. We can save the day and fall in love with the person we want, not be de-powered or married off as a prize for the square-jawed hero.

"When I was a kid, I read so much fantasy that I was convinced I was The Chosen One. My parents yelled at me for introducing my friends as my Sidekick or my Nemesis. Because heroes in fantasy can do it all—they learn magic, pick up languages in a montage, and become master swordsmen in a month on the road headed from their village to the Dark Lord's tower, winning the heart of the elven princess and besting the champion swords-man from the pointy-hat-wearing Pseudo-French king-dom along the way."

She saw a dim flicker of light coming from the back

of the room, right next to the million candle power spotlight that would have her seeing dots through the weekend. It was Alex, the host, giving her the one-minute warning.

At least she'd caught the signal this time. Last month, she hadn't even seen the timer and they'd cut her mic when she went over.

Even low on time, she plowed ahead.

"So when I was eight, confident that I was The Chosen One, I decided to begin my heroic skills acquisition. I spent six months awaiting my parents' tragic death with Wednesday Addams–level fascination.

"Thankfully, they lived, and I forged on un-orphaned. First, I tried to become a master alchemist. My parents bought me a My Little Scientist kit, but even after eight weeks, all I could do was almost blow up our garage. My older brother's bike is still stained mad-scientist red, more than fifteen years later. Whatever, it's not like he was using those eyebrows.

"So I gave up on alchemy and focused on riding—every good fantasy hero can ride, right? Except it wasn't fourteenth-century England, and I wasn't royalty, and my parents unsurprisingly did not accept my argument, in a bad British accent, that if they didn't max out their credit cards on horse-related expenses, that an evil wizard would rule the world." Leah made the sad trombone noise into the mic. That was good for a couple of chuckles.

"And that's when I knew. Sword fighting. Every good Chosen One knows their way around a sword. So I guilted my parents into enrolling me in a fencing class, and I tell you what. You have never seen someone happier than ten-year-old me running around with a kid-sized épée pretending to be Aragorn or Inigo Montoya." Leah mimed some slashes and thrusts.

"I practiced and practiced—stayed with it way longer than anything else. Even got into some tournaments. I got all the way to the finals in my division.

"And you know what happened?"

She waited a second, let the suspense build.

Another flicker of light from the back. Her time was up. Just as she was getting some momentum.

Leah stopped, turning to the audience. She'd keep practicing her blocking and timing, even if she was performing to an effective audience of one.

"What happened is I got my ass handed to me six ways from Sunday by a kid from Iowa that had been fencing since he was four.

"I was fuming after the bout. But my parents made me go congratulate him. He introduced me to his parents, and guess what? They were farmers. And the kid? Adopted.

"You never *choose* to be the Chosen One. You just *are*."

The guy in the coat nodded, his arms crossed.

"And you know what? That kid sent me a friend request two weeks ago. He's headed to the Olympics.

"But even though I never won a tournament, I found something I loved even though it was hard, even though I would never be the best. Those stories made me believe in myself. That's what fantasy means to me."

Alex approached the stage, not remotely happy with her for going over time. His little light was flashing like a raver strobe.

"But I tell you what—if you come across a farm boy and an old wizard, shiv them, take their horses, and go make your own destiny.

"Thank you, and good night!" She bowed (shallow, so as to not give the bros anything to look at), then clomped off-stage, still grumpy about acquiescing to Cal's creepy demand that all women wear heels to perform. Flats were wonderful, she loved flats. Even heels couldn't make her tall on stage, so why even pretend?

Alex gave her a falsely enthusiastic high-five, resuming his thankless job as host.

"How about that Leah Tang. Quite a kid! Keep it going now for our next comic, Kyle Jones!"

One person's solid applause and another half-dozen

golf-claps were her reward for the night.

Well, that and the free booze. Cal's one bit of generosity. Even if you washed out, open mic performers always got a drink on the house.

Leah made a beeline to the bar and ordered her customary post-gig Jack & cola. She preferred Laphroaig on the rocks, but her comps didn't go anywhere near that far. And she was expecting a whole lotta nothing in tips.

Though surprisingly, No Fat Chicks tossed a ten-dollar bill in the can Alex walked around for her. That'd pay for her cab home, at least.

"Not the best night," Inez the bartender said, mixing the drink. Inez could be counted on to enjoy the show, but she couldn't play favorites. Not since her very noticeable dislike of a misogynistic-as-hell show a few months back got her in hot water with Cal.

The bartender kept her black hair short, since she "hated ponytails worse than she hated well tequila"—an exact quote that Leah had logged away for use in a future set. Leah had a thousand little lines like that jotted across a half-dozen notebooks that she used to stitch together ideas on the whiteboard in her room.

"I think the guy in the coat was paying attention to something other than my ass."

"It's a fine ass, kid. You should be proud of it. But if it's ass they're looking for, they should be at Whistlin'

Dixie's, not here." Inez topped off Leah's drink with an extra pour of Jack.

Leah raised the drink to salute the bartender, then took a long swig.

Someone appeared to her right, and Leah turned to see No Fat Chicks, drink in hand. Up close, she saw how sloshed he was.

"That was fantastic, dude," he said, slurring. "Hot and funny. Plus," he whispered, "I'm really into reptiles and I think you'd look amazing covered in snakes."

So not only had he completely missed her point, now he was going to sloppily hit on her. Sigh.

"An impressive performance, Ms. Tang," said another voice, stepping from around No Fat Chicks's broad shoulders. It was the dude in the coat.

Perfect timing.

"Thanks, man," she said to the bro, then turned to face the guy in the coat, hoping her other admirer would get bored and wander off.

Leah saluted with her drink. "I wish a few more people here shared your perspective." She took another sip.

The drunk bro stood there like a loading cursor, trying to figure out what to say.

"Perhaps your insights might be better used elsewhere," the guy in the coat said. He reached into his pocket and pulled out a business card with a Johns Hopkins logo.

"I'm Dr. Angstrom King, Department of Comparative Literature. I run a narrative immersion laboratory, and I'm looking for new staff. I think you might be an excellent fit." King had the upper-class Yankee accent that she associated with the Ivies, but he wore it well. Some folks used that accent like a weapon, a constant reminder of their superiority.

He wasn't coming off as scary, thank goodness. And Leah knew from scary, thanks to her share of sketchy dudes trying to pick her up after sets.

Speaking of which, No Fat Chicks had lost interest and wandered off. Thank goodness.

"Immersive Narrative Laboratory?" Leah asked, looking at the business card, which announced King as a Visiting Professor of English. "Mind de-academia-ing that a bit for me?"

"My team are narrative specialists working with stories in very much the same way that your routine did. We have a big project running right now, and I could use someone with your perspective."

"I've got a job, thanks," Leah said, turning her back to King and reacquainting herself with her drink. She'd put college in her rear view several years back and was glad of it. This "Immersive Narrative Laboratory" was a load of crap if she'd ever heard of one. And while working the reception desk at the accountants' office was far from glamorous, it kept her afloat financially and didn't expect her to work overtime.

"I understand your reluctance, Ms. Tang. The Refusal of the Call is especially strong for persons of your generation. But we pay very well, and the benefits are quite hard to beat."

"Going Campbell on me isn't going to change my mind," Leah said, taking another drink, "but I could stand to hear more about the pay."

Leah looked to Inez for confirmation one way or another. "Is this guy legit?"

Inez nodded. "Word is he helped Tommy Suarez land that HBO special."

Leah froze. Oh, he was *that* kind of weirdo. The "eccentric as all get-out but really well-connected and potentially very useful" weirdo. She perked up.

Tommy hadn't made it big yet, but he'd gone straight from working the regional circuit to an HBO special, which did not happen in the normal world. And if this was the guy who helped Tommy make that jump, she could take the time to check out this "lab."

Plus, this place was tapped out, so she'd need a new lead. She'd made the rounds in the Baltimore circuit, and she was getting nowhere. She needed a break.

"You should have had Inez vouch for you in the beginning," Leah said.

"It means more if you do the asking for yourself. If you've changed your mind, I'd like to introduce you to the team tonight. And if you come along, hear me out as I explain what our team does. I'll ensure that you have a weekly gig here or at any other club in the Baltimore-DC area you want for as long as you like."

A steady gig, indefinitely. She hadn't gotten close to graduating out of the open mics. If this guy could guarantee her a steady gig, give her time to sort out her material, find an aesthetic that could connect with audiences . . . Leah tried to avoid salivating at the idea.

Leah checked her phone. "But it's eleven o'clock. Your team works that late every Thursday night?"

"Tonight we do. Shall I bring my car around?"

Leah shifted her weight from one hip to the other. She took a long swig and asked, "You have to tell me if you're going to axe murder me, right? Some kind of professorial code of conduct?"

King's expression brightened. He mimed a posh British accent. "Indeed. It's a condition of my tenure. Along with the requirement that I be absentminded and wear tweed jackets with patches."

"Well, if that's the case, sure." Leah finished off her drink and left a tip for Inez, who made the glass and bills vanish with her magic.

King lead the way and Leah followed, reassuring herself that her mace was in fact where it was supposed to be in her jacket.

The two made their way out into the ever-humid Baltimore night. King worked a key fob and a too-nice-for-a-visiting-professor Mazda came alive three spots up the street.

"Where's this lab of yours?"

King opened the door for Leah. "South of the city. Shouldn't take but twenty minutes to get there."

Leah held the door as King went to the driver's side, not quite ready to climb in and commit to doing something quite this dangerous. "And a reminder. No axe murdering."

King climbed into the car. "Ms. Tang, if I wanted to find someone to kidnap and axe murder, I'd be looking for victims that are far more trusting than you. And I wouldn't be hunting in Baltimore. Things tend to go poorly for men who look like me when we're suspected of crimes in this city."

"Point."

King started the engine, which purred to life, running quiet. "As a university professor, I specialize in the disquieting reassurance. It means that my office hours are blissfully uneventful."

The sound system turned on, leaping into an Eddie

Izzard CD. One more layer of resistance peeled off, and she took her seat.

Two

The Story Lab

TRUE TO KING'S WORD, about twenty minutes later, they arrived at a two-story-tall office building off I-97.

The car had already passed several turnoffs to nowhere in particular, so if he was going to axe murder her, he was taking the long way there. That was comforting. Sort of.

The building had a dome on one side that arched up another story's worth. IMAX, maybe? Maybe that's what he meant by narrative immersion. She could think of worse jobs than getting paid to watch IMAX documentaries about penguins and hummingbirds.

King rolled the car into a spot that read "Team Leads."

"What I'm going to show you may seem incredible, but know that it can all be explained by science. Our mission is one of exploration."

"That's not ominous at all," Leah said, stepping out of the car. On the drive over, she'd texted two different friends to check on her in an hour to make sure she was okay. Mr. and Mrs. Tang didn't raise no dumbass. Smartass, yes, but not dumb.

King opened the door with a quick scan of a passcard, revealing a stark corridor with an institutional look. The rooms were labeled innocuous things like "Archives, 1970–1979" and "Personnel Files" and odder things like "Probe Reports," "Skill-acquisition Lounge," and "Dimensional Barometric Chamber."

Her nerves had resumed assembly of a worry-henge when King threw open a set of double doors at the end of the hallway, leading into a room that looked half like the NASA command center and half like a newsroom.

The room was nearly empty, only a half-dozen of the stations filled by men and women in polo shirts, each watching several screens of TV shows, none of them immediately recognizable.

"My team is through here," King said, leading her along one side of the room. At the far wall, wide windows showed a room that looked for all the world like a hangar. If her spatial sense was working, that would be where the IMAX dome was.

King led her into another long hallway that spanned the length of the building. Part of the way down the hall, voices prompted Leah to turn and see a crash cart round the corner behind front of them. Lab-coat-and-scrubs-clad figures pushed the cart, checking the IV drip, taking pulse, and more. The patient was a white woman, blond, very banged up, and wearing an outfit that belonged at a kitschy Wild West party. The cart raced by, and King peeled off to join them, pointing to a nearby room.

"Wait in there," he said.

Leah stood befuddled for a moment as the cart and its entourage rounded a corner.

What *was* this place? A shiver ran down Leah's spine, fear tackling curiosity into a confusing melee.

The doors King had pointed to revealed a break room, and a nice one at that. It had several flat-panel TVs on the walls, treadmills with built-in screens, a full kitchen, several fridges, couches, tables, and a library in one corner.

An older Middle Eastern woman with silvery hair sat in the rocking chair amid the library. She held a massive hardcover in her lap.

Noticing Leah, the woman set her book down and stood.

"Hi," Leah said.

"You must be Leah. I'm Shirin Tehrani." Her voice was a smooth alto, welcoming and kind.

Shirin crossed, heels clicking on the floor, and extended a hand along with a warm smile. "Pleased to meet you."

"So King told you I was coming, did he?"

"Of course. He keeps us apprised of candidates and solicits our input. Your evaluations in improvisational thinking and threat responses were very impressive. You have to be quick on your toes in this job."

"Threat responses?" Leah asked. "I thought this was a lab. What is it, really? There was a crash cart or something, and King went off and said I should wait here."

Worry crossed Shirin's face, but didn't stick. Why was she so calm?

Leah's danger senses were going off. She had a few minutes left to send the all-clear text. It didn't seem like anyone was hiding axes for murdering, but they might all be delusional.

Or maybe it was a cult. A story cult? Granddaughters of Grimm or something?

"It's as he said—a narrative laboratory. This will go more smoothly if you wait for him to explain. Please help yourself to coffee or a snack or anything while you wait. But try not to worry about the woman you saw. Our medical facilities are top of the line."

Shirin's smile was gracious. The woman's whole demeanor said "classy aunt." Leah could use some classy aunts in her life. All of her aunts were back in Minnesota.

Leah looked around for some normalcy to latch on to. *Hey look, coffeemaker. Yes.* Java was needed to face the fear. "Is the coffee any good?" she asked.

"It's good for office coffee. And the granola bars are passable, if you're hungry. They're in the second drawer to the left of the fridge."

When Leah looked back, Shirin had plopped back down and was once again consumed with her book. She was acting like this wasn't weird, but it clearly was.

Leah's pulse quickened, and she tuned in to her peripheral vision, wary.

Think about the gigs, Leah, she thought, trying to find her calm.

The coffee was, in fact, passable. More importantly, it was hot. She passed on the granola bar, and walked the room, not comfortable enough to sit down when she had a hundred questions and the only other person in the building she'd met so far didn't seem interested in talking.

A few minutes later, Leah's coffee buzz was in full effect as Professor King returned. He wiped off his hands and tossed the bloodied rag in a bucket beside a waste bag.

Leah asked, "Are you going to tell me what this is all about, now? And who was that on the gurney?"

"The woman on the gurney is Mallery, a member of my team. She's being treated now. As for what this is about, why don't I just show you?" King said, his voice level. King escorted Leah to the command-room thing. Shirin put her book down and joined them.

As they entered the command room, King made straight for a woman Leah's age with thick glasses and an incredibly bright wardrobe, patterns on patterns set against a traffic cone orange shawl. She sat in a wheelchair, a complex set of monitors and two keyboards within arm's reach.

"This part is really cool," King said. "Preeti, can you bring up the orientation video on Big One, please?"

"Sure thing, boss."

The woman's hands blurred, typing at court transcriptionist speed. A moment later, one of the large screens went dark. Preeti held her over-the-ear earphones out to Leah.

She took the wireless headset, which played the opening riffs of an orchestral score like an epic movie trailer.

Earth popped up on the screen, clouds and storms and oceans and all that jazz. The screen zoomed out, showing Earth surrounded by a rough circle of red light, a dozen other worlds in fragments around it. The orbiting was replaced by circular logos—crossed revolvers, a heart, a magnifying glass, a rocket ship.

I am surrounded by crazy people right now, Leah thought, already prepping her escape strategy.

A familiar voice started to narrate. It was King.

"Stories are the DNA of the universe."

Wait, what?

"We think of life in three dimensions. With time, that makes four. Some scientists posit that we live in eleven dimensions.

"But for our purposes, there are only five that matter.

"The fifth dimension is narrative. In the fifth dimension, Earth is surrounded on all sides by worlds that are simultaneously familiar and irreducibly distinct."

The camera panned to the side, zooming in on one of the adjacent worlds. Getting closer, every bit of land area on one continent was covered by city, towers and factories, and the circuit-board of lights that reminded Leah of flying into Southern California by night.

"Each world hosts the inspiration for a narrative genre. This world inspires our stories of Science Fiction."

The world spun, resolving into shots of iconic science fiction scenes—a launching rocket, a massive laboratory filled with androids, a cityscape with flying cars, a bustling space station.

"There are dozens of others." The screen showed a Western boom town, a mine shaft entrance in the distance.

Next came a contemporary American city filled with people going about their lives. The camera moved inside a café, where every table was filled with couples. Some were awkward, stealing glances and then looking away.

Others were twitterpated. One woman was on her knee, proposing to her girlfriend. Another was having a knock-down drag-out fight.

"Romance."

The screen flipped through other worlds more quickly.

First, a fantasy kingdom, with gnomes, dwarves, and elves walking around a market town, castle towers in the background. A flourish of colorful magic erupted from the gnome's hands as a crowd looked on. It was her bit come to life.

"Fantasy."

Then the screen jumped through several more, offering views of worlds Leah pegged as noir, horror, and one world populated by pirates with shirts open to the waist, oiled chests, and tight breeches, and women in gigantic Elizabethan dresses corseted within an inch of their lives.

Finally, the screen returned to the picture of the earth, surrounded by the other worlds.

"Because of your specific skills, you've been selected to join this elite team and protect not only Earth, but dozens of other worlds, from destruction."

This was too much. Leah pulled one ear of the headset off and sniped back at King. "Are you serious? This is some Rylan Star League ridiculousness."

She started walking for the door. The playback continued. "In any system, there is entropy. When something breaks down in one of these worlds, when a story goes wrong, it ripples back on Earth.

"When a story breaches in the Western world, violence runs rampant on Earth Prime."

She looked back as she passed Preeti, starting to take off the headset. On the screen, a newspaper showed the headline "Shooting Spree in Omaha. Seventeen wounded, two dead."

Leah took the headset off entirely. "Hold up. You're telling me that broken stories affect our world? Some kind of feedback?"

"Keep watching," King said, his patience clearly wavering.

The video continued.

Leah's curiosity grabbed her, and she donned the headset again.

"Every world has a different influence on Earth."

The worlds again.

"The mission of the Genrenauts Foundation is to minimize these dangerous ripples between the worlds. When a story world goes off-track, it's our job to set it right. Using inter-dimensional vessels launched from this and other facilities around the world, teams travel to the impacted world, investigate the story breach, and put it back on-track."

The screen resolved to a logo—Earth surrounded by a dozen worlds, with "GENRENAUTS—MID-ATLANTIC ASTRODOME."

Leah took the headset off and turned to the group. Her disbelief, her desire to not be caught by some weird gotcha, took center stage.

"This is some kind of History Channel documentary, right? On after *Ancient Aliens*?"

King was nonplussed.

"Some kind of lab hazing prank or something? I thought this was going to be a touchy-feely writing job, like High Culture TwitFeed or something."

Preeti paused the playback.

"It is exactly what the pretentious video says it is," King said. "Maintaining balance between the worlds is of incalculable importance. We stand in one of several bases that monitor and respond to dimensional disturbances. There is one such disturbance right now, in the world that inspires our Western genre. One of our team has been severely injured in a failed attempt to patch the story breach, and I would like to bring you along with my team to observe as we resolve the situation."

"Tell me more about these ripples."

King had to be a professor, he had the sigh of the put-upon down pat. "When a story breaks, that breach creates a thematic-semiotic ripple effect, which crosses over from that world to our own Earth. Each of those story worlds has its own distinct signature derived from the genre it represents, and each signature has a different effect on Earth when it ripples over. Identifying and patching story breaches as quickly as possible minimizes these ripple effects and keeps the earth roughly as we know it."

Heady stuff. No wonder they hired a lit professor to run the team.

Leah made the "go on" hand gesture. "And now, unpack that one more time like I'm stupid. Because this still sounds crazypants."

Another sigh, this one more exasperated. "Right now, a story is broken in the Western story world. Western world's signature is about violence, order vs. lawlessness, and taking the law into your own hands. Do you remember the shooting in Vegas yesterday?" King asked.

"Yeah."

"That was only the first of several identified ripple events over the last forty-eight hours since the breach began."

King turned to Preeti. "Bring up the news feeds."

Preeti tabbed through to another program, and pulled up a news site.

The headlines read:

VIGILANTE SHOOTER KILLS FIVE BURGLARS

IN EVANSVILLE, IN

UNIDENTIFIED GUNMAN SHOOTS SEVEN IN WASHINGTON PUBLIC PARK. ALL IN CRITICAL CONDITION. GUNMAN STILL AT LARGE.

SWAT RAID GONE SOUTH: FIVE OFFICERS IN CRITICAL CONDITION.

"And if we don't fix this story breach," King said, "the shootings will continue. The whole world will shift. More people will take the law into their own hands, will take what they think they deserve by force."

King jabbed a finger at the screens. "That's what I mean by thematic-semiotic resonance. A story breaks, and then people die, lives are ruined. I need to send a team to Western world and fix the story now. I brought you in because I thought you could help. Do you want to critique stories your whole life, or would you rather fix them?"

"Hold up. I have friends in Vegas, and you're telling me they might have gotten killed because of some broken story in a whole other world?"

"Those are the stakes, Leah. Now it's time to make a decision. You have ten minutes."

King turned and made his way out of the room, apparently done with the conversation.

Shirin watched him go, saying, "He gets what we'd call 'passionate' about the job."

Leah turned to watch the news feeds. She'd heard about the shootings, but had blamed it on the social media age, where a small story can become a huge story within an hour.

"So you're script doctors, but for real worlds? And somehow also dimensional cops?" Leah said, trying to parse the unbelievable.

Shirin smiled. "That depends on what you mean by real. The people on these worlds have their own lives, their own desires, but they are bound by the rules of their world. We help keep their worlds running as they're meant to. It's the best job you could ask for. Adventure, excitement, a new challenge every mission."

Preeti had turned back to her workstation, watching three screens, each showing a view of what had to be the Western world—Old West buildings, saloons, cowboys on horseback, and a trio of Native American men from a Great Plains tribe trading with a merchant on a street corner.

"So how finely sliced do the genre worlds get? Is there a Slasher world, a sports movie world?" Leah asked.

Shirin gestured to the wall of screens. Looking closer,

she started to pick out different worlds. Each pack of 3x3 screens seemed to show one world, but with different styles. "Each world has one umbrella genre which sets the tone for that world. Fantasy world has dark fantasy, epic fantasy, and sword and sorcery, all on different continents far removed from one another. Slasher would be a region in Horror world. Sports stories happen all over, but something like *A League of Their Own* would go to Women's Fiction world.

"I hate that label, by the way," Shirin added, "but unless we convince the High Council to rename it, that's what it is." That sounded like an argument that had gone around the block more than a few times. "I guarantee you that this will be more exciting than answering phone calls, scheduling meetings, and processing expense reports."

"Don't knock expense reports. There's a kind of magic in paying bills with other people's money," Leah said.

Shirin said, "I could see the appeal in that. But what we do is storytelling at the highest possible stakes, determining the fate of individuals, nations, and entire worlds all at once."

Gulp. "No pressure, right?"

Shirin nodded. The woman seemed to be shooting straight, not sugarcoating it to get her to sign her soul away.

But curiosity wouldn't let her just walk away. She might as well see how deep the rabbit hole went before deciding whether to take the leap.

Leah waved at the screens. "So, what does it take to cross the dimensional barriers or whatever you do?"

"For that, we go to the Hangar."

———————

Bakhtin Hangar contained several berths with snub-nosed rocket ships under repair and reconstruction, as well as launching stations.

One of the ships stood on end, scaffolding and a set of stairs attached—for maintenance, most likely. The ship was twenty feet tall, with a glass port on the top, and a larger hatch near the back. Techs in red jumpsuits surrounded the nearest ships, running diagnostics, moving hoses, and generally making with the busy.

King watched the scurrying preparations, tapping through menus on a tablet.

"So you cross dimensions in that?" Leah asked.

"Exactly," King said.

"So why haven't I heard about the weird rocket launches by BWI?"

"Because they never cross above that hoop. These ships travel in the fifth dimension, they're designed to traverse the boundaries between Earth Prime and the narrative dimensions. And this one is about to launch. What do you say?"

"I say this is still totally bonkers."

"That's fair. But the offer stands—come with us, and you'll have a steady comedy gig for as long as you want it."

"So what are the chances that I get killed in your little excursion?" Leah asked.

"Not at all likely. I'd give it a seven percent chance. Only three percent if you follow all of my directions."

"The fact that you know those percentages without thinking makes me think that the actual odds are way worse." Leah looked at the ship, at the dome above, and thought about the drudgery awaiting her at the office tomorrow.

It was totally ridiculous that this place was even here, right under everyone's noses. A whole multiverse of possibility and semio-thematic thingamawhatsits and professional dimensional story doctors jumping between worlds as regularly as corporate troubleshooters.

The smart thing to do would be to get them to call her a cab, text her friends that she was coming home, and forget this whole thing. She could try the Attic again, promise to use different material, and keep trying, keep grinding until she got a break. That's what made sense.

Watching the techs cluster around the ship, King barking orders, rushing the team to move faster, Leah imagined what that normal life would be like.

Banality by day, frustration by night. Weekends in coffeeshops writing material, late nights dying on the stage again and again.

Or . . . this. This bizarre, dangerous job with infinite possibility. And, even if she didn't like it—wasn't suited or whatever—she could take the gig. King had delivered for Tommy Suarez, and Inez vouched for him. And wasn't a steady gig worth an evening of bizarreness?

She thought about the woman on the gurney, the mention of "casualties," weighed it against the chance to fly in a rocket ship, to see impossible vistas, to take her passion for stories and use it to make a real difference. That is, if all of this was real. But she'd never know unless she gave it a shot.

And there was her answer.

Leah popped off a quick "all clear" text to her friends as she walked toward the rocket.

"Hey, King," she shouted. "Do I get to wear a cool bubble helmet?"

"Not this time," King said, turning with the hint of a smile. "First, there is some very exciting paperwork for you to fill out."

Much less cool.

But still, spaceship.

Three

Blast Off

LEAH HELD ON FOR DEAR LIFE, sitting with her back to the floor, gravity pulling like a tilt-a-whirl, minus the spinning.

King was at the helm. Shirin had the copilot seat, calling out sensor data. Leah sat in the second row, alone, with boxes of supplies secured behind her.

The ship rocked and rattled at a dull roar. Colors kaleidoscoped across the windshield like an acid trip mixed with a music visualizer. Leah tried to keep her regretfully greasy dinner down as the ship lurched and shook.

"What's with the rattling?" she yelled, distracting herself from her fear by complaining—a tactic she borrowed from pre-K kids everywhere.

"It's dimensional turbulence," King said, his voice lacking its usual level calm. "The dimensions rub up against one another more sometimes than others, and that friction disturbs our passing in the fifth dimension."

"That sounds crappy." She stopped for a moment to consider. "And yet kinda cool. Has it ever killed anyone?" she asked, not really wanting to know the answer, but fear was in the driver's seat, and the question was out before she could swallow it.

"Not often," Shirin said, her knuckles white on the sides of her seat.

A strap broke behind her, and Leah saw gear tumbling to the ground. A bag spilled old-timey Western clothes—ponchos, starched shirts, dusters, and chaps. Another bundle went clang with the sound of metal on metal as a rolled-up tube of guns toppled to the floor.

"The universe is coming undone back here," Leah said. She caught Shirin looking on, the older woman's eyes evaluating the damage, worry showing through a hastily applied mask of calm.

"If you get me killed before I even get to see *Westworld*, I'm going to be ridiculously pissed-off."

King worked the controls, hauling back on a lever and slamming a button. The ship lurched to the left, and a few bumpy moments later, the turbulence faded. The windshield view-screen resolved to a flat white, which then receded into a horizon, a sun-drenched desert at high noon.

"Can we skip that part on the way back?" Leah asked, taking deep breaths and locking her vision on the horizon to try to reassemble her shattered equilibrium. They were pointed up, gravity tugging on her back.

"Seconded," said Shirin.

King's smile was meant to be encouraging. Her stomach was still too sloshy for it to help. "That's one hurdle you've already made it past. Fascinating, no?"

"The light show was impressive, but I could have done without the rock tumbler ride."

"Tumblers take off the rough edges, don't they?" King gave a wry smile. Shirin rolled her eyes as she unbuckled.

"Why do we have to travel with our backs to the ground? Or is dangling from one's seat considered a perk?"

"Now she's getting it." King unbuckled, then adeptly climbed out of the chair, dropped to the chair beside Leah, and reached over to help her out of her seat.

"I got it, I got it." Leah swatted at his hand, working the X-cross straps that had kept her mostly stable in the seat during the crossing.

"Shirin, see to the gear."

The woman descended a column of rails at the side of the ship. Leah tested the strength of the rails, then followed.

King said, "Now that we've arrived, here's what you need to know: to do our jobs and keep the worlds stable, we need to make as little an impact here as possible.

We're surgeons, not sawbones. We nudge the story back on track, and do it from the shadows whenever possible. If the people of this world realize that they're being messed with by outsiders, then even more stories will go off-track, and the whole problem will only compound until we're all quite screwed."

Leah climbed onto the stairs and made her way down to the pile of rucksacks. "Tread softly, got it. But won't we stand out regardless? Westerns aren't exactly known for their diversity. Black guy, Asian woman, and a Middle Eastern woman wander into a saloon, people are going to notice. And then make a joke. And then shoot us."

King nodded. "Sad truth is, you're right. That's why we have these." He gestured to the Marshal's pin on his jacket. "This is a Personal Phase Manipulator, or PPM. They let us project an illusion and fit in to the story worlds. We'll look like any other three lily-white red-blooded cowfolks. We try to only use them on worlds where our operatives wouldn't otherwise be able to move unnoticed. Here, the various historical regions on Romance world, and so on."

"Anywhere that the three of us would get run out of town if we showed up looking like ourselves," Leah said.

"Exactly. That's why Mallery and Roman went first in this world," King said. "The Phase Manipulators are incredibly expensive and sometimes unreliable, so we try to minimize the need for them."

"That and Western world is usually one of the most dormant, the most stable," Shirin said. "There hasn't been a genre-redefining Western for years. The breaches here tend to be small."

Leah said, "So all the racist storytelling tropes happen in these worlds: black guys *do* always die first in Horror world, beautiful white people are ninety-five percent of the leads in Romance world while the 'ethnic' friends get paired off with one another in the credits—that kind of thing?"

"Pretty much, yes." King helped Shirin sort out their gear while Leah looked on. "Thematic-semiotic resonance is a two-way street. The way we tell stories manifests in the story worlds. The dominant narrative here is reflected on the genre world. Any given world has some room for minority narratives and counternarratives, but those are just as marginalized."

"Counternarratives. Like parodies?"

"Parodies, deconstructions, feminist or antiracist interventions into the genre, and so on."

Shirin walked by, a bag over each shoulder. "We should probably save the literary theory lecture for after the mission, Professor." She put a hand on Leah's arm. "Go ahead and get changed. The less work the Phase Manipulators have to do to make you fit in, the more reliable they are."

Leah gestured to the ship. "What about this thing? It's a bit more conspicuous than the Minority Musketeers riding into town."

"The ship has its own Phase Manipulator," King said. "It projects the image of something that makes sense in the world—like a boarded-up ranch house or a rock outcropping. Due to the size difference and the fact that it's inorganic, the phase shift is more stable."

"Because technobabble, got it," Leah said. "Glad to hear the chameleon circuit's not broken."

Shirin draped a heavy leather coat over Leah's arms, ignoring the reference. "This will make you look bigger than you are. We need to look dangerous. The best way to blend in on this world here is to come off as big and bad. Normal folks don't get in the way of people they consider to be threatening."

King opened the hatch, heading outside to give Shirin and Leah their privacy.

———

Leah adjusted her ten-gallon hat, looking in the mirror bracketed to the inside of the ship's hatch.

With her Phase Manipulator on, Leah saw a stranger before her. Leah moved, and in the mirror, a white man with Norse coloration echoed her. The illusion had sandy-blond hair, an angular face, and hair shorter than she'd had since she cut her own hair as a six-year-old.

The illusory man had Leah's build, so she wouldn't have to worry about people looking her "in the eye" at her forehead or her chest. The whole thing had the feel of LARPing an episode of *Quantum Leap* by wearing a virtual reality rig.

She turned away and looked back, catching her "self" out of the corner of her eye. If she was going to keep up this act, she would need to not be startled by seeing this illusion casually in washrooms or watering holes or whatever reflective surfaces were at hand.

Having to travel in whitewashed drag in order to not get harassed wasn't exactly what she'd call comforting, but the fascinating bizarreness of having a full-body illusion was fairly distracting from the unfairness of it all.

"Adjusted yet?" came Shirin's voice from behind her.

Shirin's cover illusion was that of a grizzled white woman of about sixty. She had a time-worn face and bone-white hair.

"This is weird, right?" Leah said, watching her hands as she talked. "I mean, we're wearing illusory white people. This is straight-up science-fictional future shock weird."

Leah put on her hat, which was two sizes too big. It

dropped right down onto her nose, blocking her vision. She flicked the brim and the hat eased back so she could see, weighing heavy on her ears.

"It's weird, but things were worse when we tried to go without the PPMs."

"So, how do I look?"

Shirin doled out another one of her classy aunt smiles. "Not quite dangerous, but it'll do." Shirin bent down and reached into another bag. She came out with a leather belt holding two holstered revolvers. "This will help with the dangerous part."

"I'm not a big gun fan," Leah said, her hand drooping as she took the weight of the belt.

"You don't have to like them, but for now, you definitely have to wear them." Shirin strapped on her own gun belt. She drew each of the guns in turn, checking the wheel and action.

"I checked yours before we went. Leave them be for now if you're not comfortable."

"I'll do that. I'm a whole lot of uncomfortable, and kind of wishing I'd taken a nap today before my set.

"Also, why isn't your illusion a dude?" Leah asked.

Shirin flinched, hurt crossing her face. Leah was about to open her mouth to apologize, but Shirin cut her off.

"I spent more than twenty years pretending to be a

boy. That's enough for several lifetimes."

"Sorry, what?" Leah asked.

Shirin dropped her shoulders, taking a breath. "I'm trans. I left Iran after the revolution in '79, when it became very clear that women like me were especially unwelcome."

Ah. Leah shut her mouth. "Sorry. I didn't know. Didn't mean to . . ."

Shirin raised a hand. Her forgiving smile wiped away some of the awkwardness. "No worries. I'm old enough that folks here won't police me quite as much as they would a spring chicken like you. Just remember to speak at the bottom of your register so you can pass for a boy without the PPM having to do it for you. Lean into the drawl and you'll be fine. And remember, here you're Lee, and I'm Atlas Jane. Now let's disembark and put this bit of awkwardness behind us, why don't we?"

"Yes, please."

———

The hatch opened as Shirin aka Atlas Jane let the harsh desert sun back in. King stood on watch adorned in a brown leather vest and slacks, a bandolier across one shoulder, a shotgun resting on the other.

"We're about a mile outside the town," King said, gesturing off into the distance, beyond some dunes. His illusion was of a black-haired Germanic white guy, grizzled enough to wear the mantle of a Marshal.

They'd arrived in scrublands, setting down at the base of one of a set of rolling hills. There were mountains off in the other direction. Cacti spattered the landscape, along with the light scrub vegetation. The view could have come from one of a hundred soundstages at MGM or any of the Studio's other golden-age Western sets.

Leah climbed down out of the ship, the boots pinching her feet. Such were the joys of being a five-wide. Shirin said she'd had to guess on the fly when they were packing, and next time she'd get tailored gear.

The earth dusted as she touched down, and she could feel the heat sucking all the moisture out of her skin.

She took a breath, the air dry, sun beating down like it was being paid. All that was missing was a tumbleweed.

And there we go, she thought, seeing one roll and bounce by on a gust of wind.

"Lead on, pardner." Leah tipped her hat, her voice as low as she could take it. King furrowed his brow and started walking.

Shirin leaned into Leah. "You're his new best friend."

Leah responded, sotto voce, "Hey, he hired me from a comedy club. Don't know what he was expecting."

"I was expecting that you would be a natural at this,"

King said over his shoulder. "Let's see if I'm right."

Walking into the town, Leah could almost see the cardboard behind the storefronts. It was every Western town from every movie brought to life, with washerwomen, mud-stained miners, vest-wearing gentlemen, prim and proper schoolmarms, and more.

She had to contain her sense of wonder, the mix of excitement and worry at seeing the tropes of a genre brought to life and plopped right in front of her. She held her hat in place as she craned her head up, scanning the buildings, squinting her eyes to make out what looked like an office for a mine in the distance, beside the ridge of rocks that stood at the town's back.

But this wasn't a happy-bouncy Western town, townfolk and ranchers greeting one another with tipped hats and the frontier hospitality of people who were all on the edge of something new together.

This town was scared.

Mothers hurried their children along from storefront to storefront, watching the horizon over their shoulder. Ranch hands stayed close by their livestock. Leah's eyes found the bank (inventively labeled "Bank and Trust"), and suddenly understood. The windows had been busted in, the door swung on one hinge, and the wooden walls had bullet-holes, as did the storefronts opposite and beside the bank.

There'd been a shootout here, or her name wasn't Montana Lee. If she was going to be Lee, and Shirin was Atlas Jane, she should get to be Montana Lee. Leah hadn't played Montana Lee since she was seven and living in the Twin Cities, but the genre-tastic sensory overflow brought back those memories, games of cops-and-robbers fueled by classic films and their glorious parodies.

Her friend Cenisa had been the sheriff, because Mel Brooks had proven that black sheriffs were cooler than the grizzled old white ones. But Montana Lee did not do karate. Or kung fu. She was a gunslinger. The best gun in the West from the Far East.

The memory left her in the right mind-set for the world, remembering the diction and drawl, the swagger that came from being bowlegged from riding and wearing boots for too long.

"The shootout was here, but the bandits are gone," Leah said, taking in the street with Shirin and King from their vantage point at the end of Main Street. "So where do we pick up the story?"

"First, we find Roman. He'll be there," King said, nodding toward the saloon, which was indicated by a gaudily painted sign showing a petticoats-laden blonde sipping from a frothy mug in a not-at-all-suggestive manner.

"This place is really on-the-nose," Leah said as an aside to Shirin.

"There's no genre awareness here. All of the tropes, the archetypes, they're just a way of life. You've got to roll with it, use it. We come to these places and we can see two steps ahead—it gives us the edge."

"I'm so paralyzed by low-hanging comedy fruit that I cannot even."

"Then I'll even, and you stay odd," King said, walking across the street to the saloon.

At least King was holding to the rule that all bosses were required to pun.

The head Genrenaut pushed open the swinging doors and stood astride the threshold for a moment, cutting an impressive silhouette with his shotgun over his shoulder and his hat seeming to take up the whole doorway.

Now *that* was an entrance. *Guess that's why he's the boss.*

Leah found herself taking mental notes, partially as a distancing technique to avoid cracking up, part because the world was so perfectly a thing unto itself. Foucault and Plato would go gonzo with this place.

King walked straight over to a booth, and Shirin followed, Leah close behind.

Entering the saloon, Leah felt a dozen sets of eyes on her, narrowed eyes below brimmed hats sizing "him" up, not in the piece of meat way she got walking by a construction site or frat or many other places.

They were getting his measure, deciding whether "he" was a threat. In the heavy coat, with her hair pulled up, and the PPM doing its job, her disguise seemed to hold up.

The attention was still intrusive, but it felt a whole hell of a lot less creepy than being ogled on the street by a bunch of construction workers. Also, this time she was armed. The guns she ignored, but the knife in her boot was reassuring.

But the size-up wasn't all only for macho reasons. There was a hint of fear at the edge of people's movements. This town had been shaken, and bad.

A tall man with sun-beaten skin sat in the corner booth, a rifle propped up beside him. He played the "don't stab yourself" game with a bowie knife, moving just fast enough to be scary. He left the knife stuck in the table and tipped his hat back as King approached the table.

This would be Roman, then.

He slid to the side and made room. There was an all-but-empty bottle of beer on the table, and a fresh one waiting beside a worn and smeared newspaper that looked like it'd been read thirty times.

Roman was probably over six feet tall, though it was always hard to tell when someone was seated. He had a heroic square jaw and corded muscle that showed through Western garb that had seen long and hard use. Of the four of them on Western world, he looked the most like a gunslinger.

He fit into the scene, but it was almost like his gravity was greater than the men around him. *Could the people here tell if someone was from a story world versus Earth? What did it mean to be of a story world?* She kept it together, thinking of the steady stand-up gig. Stay out of trouble, and one day's worth of sightseeing would pay off for years to come.

And it wasn't like she'd ever been on a job interview this bizarre or fascinating. Though once she'd been asked to sit in a room and work on logic puzzles with three other candidates while they were being observed through a one-way mirror for "leadership skills." That had been one weird summer camp.

"This must be the new recruit," Roman said with an Afrikaans accent. That'd explain the name. She didn't know many American born-and-bred Roman De Jagers. On the other hand, she'd never lived in Dutch Pennsylvania, so who knew?

"Around here, folks call me Lee," she said, offering a hand. They shook, but Roman didn't make eye contact. He sat back down as King, Shirin, and Leah filled the booth.

"Any sight of the Williamson gang?" King asked.

Roman shook his head. "They said they'd be back in two days for the rest of the bank's money. Word in town says their horses could barely trot, they were so laden down. Folks are scurrying, trying to settle their affairs and leave on tomorrow's train. Some of the bank staff rode off with as much as they could carry an hour ago. Unless we can give these folks hope, this place will be a ghost town by the time the Williamsons get back."

"Miners and ranchers both?"

"The ranchers are threatening to take their stock to the next town over, sixty miles north." Roman talked only to King, and even so, never made eye contact. The gunslinger's gaze stayed locked on the street, watching through the windows. "The miners can just head one stop down the rails to another operation. There's only silver here, no gold. The place is, in reality, perfectly vulnerable, but this isn't how the story's supposed to go. You can feel it in the air. It's not just fear. The whole world's ten degrees off-course."

King waved to the room, his voice low as they slid out of character and into story analysis or whatever it was they did in the field. "The best way to tell when a part of the story is off-track is to look at the edges of things. If someone—or some*thing*—has gone off-track, their story momentum diverted or disrupted—there's an effect at the edges, like their borders have been chewed on, or shredded. Sometimes it manifests as a fading or another form of discoloration. The effect varies by world and by story. Here, you often see colors filtered through sepia tones."

"What? That's . . . weird. So it's like Pleasantville in reverse. People lose their color or something?" Leah asked.

"Sometimes, yes. No one here can see it. It's only visible to Genrenauts, not folks from the story world itself. It takes certain detached concentration, like learning to see Magic Eye pictures. Be on the lookout, but don't go scaring anyone by staring at them like they're on fire."

"Got it. Stare, but don't stare. This probably isn't a good time to admit that I was never any good at Magic Eyes."

"No, I'd suggest you keep that to yourself," King said.

"So, where's our survivor?" Shirin asked, moving the conversation along.

Roman pulled the knife out of the table and sheathed it at his hip. "Frank Mendoza. He's here somewhere. I've been asking around, but most everyone's clammed up tight. Maybe you can get more out of people."

Shirin stole Roman's beer and drained it. "I'm already there. Come along, this will be fun," Shirin said to Leah as she stood. The older woman made her way to the bar, an exaggerated sway in her hips, her whole body language opening up like a sunflower. Where Leah had to move to mask her femininity, Shirin embraced it. She wove through the saloon, doling out compliments, leaning over poker games, and breaking the ice like an arctic steamliner.

So, that's why she's here, Leah observed. Roman's B.A., King's Hannibal, and Shirin's the Face.

But those weren't Western archetypes. *How did they fit in here?* Mapping the team members to the genre, King would be the Marshal, Roman the Gunslinger, and Shirin was what? The Woman Who Can Actually Fight? The Kindly but Tough Matron, more like. Already they were straining the confines of the genre, though her knowledge of Westerns had never moved much beyond the playground scenarios. And where did that leave her, archetype-wise? *I don't want to be the Kid. I'm always the Kid.*

And if they were supposed to stay in the shadows while also fixing a story, what roles could they really play? Maybe it wasn't about what archetype you fit so much as what impact you had. Make a difference wearing the hat of a Gunslinger, but not so much that people call you the hero. That made sense. Mostly.

"Come on, Kid," Shirin said, waving Leah over to join her at the bar.

Leah cut a straighter path through the crowd, avoiding contact as actively as Shirin had embraced it. But it was easy to move in the woman's wake once she'd swayed the mood of the room.

The saloon was almost all men—no schoolmarms, washerwomen, or other acceptable women archetypes present. Nothing but the working girls on the stairs. But Shirin made her way through the crowd on sheer determination and craftiness.

Leah took a stool beside Shirin at the bar. "I can't imagine what you're like at dinner parties." Behind the bar stood a thick-set man in black clothes and a white apron. He had the wispy echo of hair clinging to his polished head, and his hands were busy pouring whiskey in Shirin's bartenderly conjured glass.

"This fella with you, ma'am?" the bartender asked. Shirin nodded, all bright smiles and steady ease.

"One for me, thanks," Leah said, not wanting to look soft on her first day on this bizarre adventure that purported to be a job.

So far, Leah would have paid for the experience. Her mind galloped off into imagining the other story worlds, the narrative sightseeing she could do in a Diana Wynne Jones–esque Fantasyland or Hard Boiled-opolis.

Shirin brought Leah back to the present by raising a toast.

"To new friends."

Leah raised her own glass to match. Shirin downed her drink like a pro. Never one to be outdone when it came to shots (though often one to be carried home after them), she drank as well.

The rotgut burned like napalm going down. The booze made her wistful for the generic paint-thinner-grade stuff she and friends had drunk in high school before any of them knew better.

Leah set her glass down and gave Shirin a questioning stink-eye, interrupted by coughing.

"When in Rome."

"He's the Roman," Leah said, gesturing back to the corner.

"Exactly. He fits in perfectly." Shirin spun on the stool and leaned back on the bar, taking in the room.

"Now where would you begin if you were looking for information?" she said at a whisper. "Remember, think genre tropes."

"Shouldn't I be looking for the sepia thing?"

"That comes with time. And if you rely on the micro, you can lose the macro. Let's start with what you already know—story. We can develop the rest later."

Leah scanned the room, trying to read it like a crowd before a set.

There were ten tables and five booths. A small elevated stage filled the wall opposite the bar, with a player piano and dingy red curtains and trim. A trio of dancers in red and black finery perched at the far side of the bar, turned in toward one another to ward off drunken advances.

Another set of women draped themselves around the railing heading upstairs, all painted to the nines—those would be the working girls, though for all Leah knew the women might do both. The saloon patrons were divided between miners, ranchers, and folks Leah supposed were the town drunks or vagabonds. Most draped over tables in a stupor, their tables cluttered by half-empty bottles of the same rotgut that would be plaguing her, later on.

"First things first, I'd ask the bartender. If he's like the ones I know, they keep a close eye on who comes and goes. After that, I'd look around for any friends or family the guy had in town—if anyone's left."

Shirin said, "Good. Now you watch the room while I talk to the bartender. See if anyone listens in. Chances are, anyone close to Frank is going to have their ear to the ground to see if anyone is after him."

With that, the older woman spun on the stool and

raised her glass to the bartender. "Another round, please, Ollie."

His attention ensnared, Shirin continued. "You seen Frank Mendoza since the shootout?"

A shadow passed over Ollie's face. He looked down, settling his gaze onto the bottles and glasses.

Leah turned from Ollie to look across the room to the team, focusing on the edges of her peripheral vision. Thankfully, she had years of experience, thanks to keeping an eye on hecklers and skeevy people on the street, dating all the way back to being an early blossomer as a kid.

The working girls continued their chatter, mugging for the room, half-paying attention to everyone and no one at the same time. The gamblers were getting almost raucous, the pall of the Williamson gang deferred temporarily by drink and the promise of a big win.

Nothing yet.

The bartender said, "Ain't seen Frank since the fight, no. Who's asking?"

Shirin answered, "Someone who isn't about to let the Williamson gang stampede right through this town. But if I'm going to do that, I need to know how the Williamsons fight. And for that, I need Frank. If you haven't seen him, who has?"

"You with that big fella in the corner?"

Shirin raised her voice, talking to the bartender but clearly meaning to be heard by more. "That I am. He's the fastest draw you or I will ever see, and I've been all over this county, from the Mississippi to the Big Easy and up through the plains. And he don't cotton to bullies. If someone here knows Frank, it'd be for the good of the town for us to meet him."

The bartender continued. "Don't suppose I know anyone who ran with Frank, aside from his poor brother. They came to town 'bout a month ago, hadn't made many friends."

While the bartender dissembled, one of the working girls descended the stairs by a step. She was younger, no more than twenty, with amber-brown skin and night-black hair done up at the top, ringlets at the back. She leaned against the railing nearest to the bar, disengaged from her companions. She was attempting (poorly) trying to mask her intent by pointing her face toward the stage. But her eyes were fixed on the bar.

Leah figured the girl gave herself away because she wasn't comfortable in the clothes, fidgeting and adjusting every few seconds. New to the job, most like. Leah adjusted her archetypal assessment of the girl and made a judgment call.

Leah nudged Shirin with her elbow and whispered, "Nine o'clock, on the stairs."

Shirin leaned back from the bar and said, "Well, if no one else in town knew him, I guess we're on our own. Thank you kindly." Shirin set her drink down, her sigh matching the sound of glass on wood. "And in that case, I'm going to need some help getting my friend to relax. Who do I talk to about the working girls?"

Leah spun on the stool to watch Shirin work, her target already pegged.

"You'll want to talk to Miss Sarah, there. She takes care of folks what need relaxing." On the stairs, a woman about Shirin's age nodded to Shirin. Her dress was fine, if worn. That'd be the madam, then.

After buying another whiskey and a beer to go with it, Shirin slid off of her stool and led Leah back to the corner. Leah followed, and the group re-formed at the booth.

"The Kid here pegged our lead," Shirin said. "The youngest working girl on the stairs was a bit too curious when I was asking around about Frank."

Roman joined in. "Mallery suspected that Frank and Juan were hiding a sister."

King said, "What's your play?"

Shirin slid the beer over to Roman, replacing the one she'd taken. "I mentioned that Roman here was in need of some comfort. The Kid takes Roman to ask for the girl, and then Roman goes up to pump her for information."

"But thankfully, nothing else," Roman said.

Leah said, "If I knew you better, this is where I would make a joke, but I don't want to offend."

King pointed a finger at Leah. "And once he's up there, I need you to keep an eye on him. Establish and maintain direct visual or aural contact. We don't like to send agents into unknown situations without backup nearby. Roman can handle himself, so this is a test for you. I want to see how you think on your feet."

Roman took a long swig from the drink, then slid out of the booth. "Come on, Kid. Let's go get me a woman," Roman said in a low voice, hamming it up for her.

"Me, too? Kinky," Leah joked.

"I'm too embarrassed to ask for myself, so you get to go with me and make sure the girl is nice. I haven't been with anyone since my wife died, so you're being careful on my behalf."

"That's a cover, right?"

"Got it," Roman said, tipsily swaggering across the room, though he'd been stone-cold sober in the booth. Were the whole team actors, then? "King says you did improv. Just roll with it."

Leah made a show of steadying Roman, accompanying him to the stairs. Leah looked up to Miss Sarah, a regal woman who held herself like the dust and grit of the town was simply not allowed to wear her down.

"You'd be Miss Sarah?" Leah asked, pitching her voice low.

The woman nodded. "I am. How can my girls help you?"

"Why don't you sit down, Roman?" Leah said, making a gesture of lowering the big man to a seat. Leah took a step up and leaned in to whisper the story that Roman had made up on the fly while the woman fanned herself, masking her lips.

"I see," Sarah said. "Does he have a preference? Girls?" She leaned in. "Boys?"

"If he's going to get over his wife, I think he'd need a woman's attentions, Miss Sarah. I caught him stealing glances at the young lady at the top of the stairs. . . ."

Miss Sarah turned and beckoned the woman down.

The younger woman questioned her every move, not confident about taking up the space she occupied. Seeing her closer, she was maybe eighteen. Not out of adolescence, with all of the self-consciousness that came with it.

Improv had been what helped Leah get past that. Presumably, sex work could do it, too, but if the girl had come into town with her brothers, she wouldn't have been at the business long. But how did it work in the genre world? Was it the sanitized version of sex work from the movies and books, or was it actual early modern sex work, warts and all?

"This is Maribel. She'll take care of your friend."

Leah repeated Roman's made-up backstory to Maribel, who nodded.

"I'll do my best, Miss Sarah."

Maribel descended to Roman, who had stuck to character, tipsily sulking at his empty table.

"Come on, Roman. Miss Maribel would like to speak with you upstairs." Leah mimed helping him to his feet. Thankfully, Roman did all the lifting himself, because Leah was pretty sure she wouldn't have been able to get him to his feet on her own.

Roman got one hand on the railing, and Maribel looped her lace-gloved hand through his other arm, guiding him up the stairs.

They stopped at the landing and Leah turned to Sarah, who watched the pair move while smiling for the crowd. Her respect for the madam kept ratcheting up. She was the best version of the archetype brought to life.

"Uh, Miss Sarah. There's one more thing. I wanted to ask if I might wait by the door, make sure he goes through with it and stops moping all over our campfires."

Miss Sarah crossed her arms. "My girls are plenty encouraging on their own."

Leah tried to improv a reason why the madam should let her go up anyway, and the only good ones involved paying for her own company, which she decided against.

"Fair enough." Leah stepped back, starting to turn.

Think. Think. Think.

Ah.

"You got an outhouse? That whiskey goes straight through me."

"Out back, up against the rocks," Miss Sarah said.

Leah tipped her hat to the madam. She "helped" Roman up the stairs, and then made herself heard as she came right back down and left by the front door.

The street was almost totally empty, save for some people packing wagons and loading saddlebags.

Rounding the corner to head for the outhouse back, Leah put a hand to her ear to activate the comm. "Roman's upstairs with Maribel, but I couldn't get permission to go up and watch his back. Finding another spot now."

King's voice answered her. "Just act casual. The PPM will help you blend into the background if you let it."

"Got it."

Through the comm, Leah overheard Roman and Maribel exchanging niceties. The Afrikaaner was playing coy, inviting Maribel to be more active to draw him out. Problem was, it wasn't working. So they were mostly not talking. Leah imagined the awkwardness of two fully clothed strangers looking at each other in a bedroom, saying mostly nothing. She'd had dates like that.

The saloon's backyard rolled right into a rock outcropping twelve feet high, a natural wind block. Leah found the outhouse no problem, but what she was looking for was another way in or upstairs. There was a back door to the saloon, which she bet had a stairwell for staff to supplement the grand stairway in the main room.

A quick peek in the window showed a kitchen where off-duty girls sat eating and chatting. No way she'd be getting in there. As she began to pull her head back, something caught her eye.

The cook, a younger man, looked familiar. Really familiar. As in, family resemblance familiar.

Bingo.

Leah scooted away from the back door and took a long arc to the tree, plotting a path up to the first-floor awning that stretched along the back wall of the saloon. More than enough for her to crawl along, if she were industrious. Since she'd been climbing trees and jungle gyms since she was three, the answer to that question was a confident yes. Sitting up in the tree would get her close enough for visual contact, if the angle was right and if Roman was on this side of the building. And she bet she could get to the window in about thirty seconds if she had to.

Leah angled her path to the outhouse to make sure

she wasn't being watched as she moved to the back side of the tree. Then, using skills earned with many skinned knees and sprained ankles, she scurried up, perching herself among the leaves and finding a stable position with a view of the rooms. The shades were drawn, but they were all light-colored, and still yielded silhouettes.

She had eyes on three rooms from her angle. One was clearly not Roman and Maribel, as the silhouetted figures were already very much in the middle of things. But two other pairs were in the "just talking" phase.

"In position. Roman, if you can stand up now, I'll confirm your location."

A figure in one of the rooms stood, taking a step forward.

"Confirmed. I have eyes on," Leah said.

"Well done," King said. "Now stay put, and don't get caught."

"One more thing," Leah added, happy that King couldn't see her self-satisfied smile. "I'm pretty sure our sole survivor is working in the kitchen."

A moment went by, and Roman said, "Is that so?" presumably waiting for a chance to say the same line for both conversations.

With no one around, there was no reason to hide her proud grin. "Thought you might want to know."

Leah settled in, getting comfortable in the tree. The

flaky bark made that hard, but she'd spent many an afternoon reading in trees. *Okay, big guy, it's all you,* she thought, locking in on Roman as the pair continued to talk.

———————

Roman stood two paces from the bed. The room was practically hotel-bare, without even the faux-homey gestures that chain hotels indulged in to show that they cared. Maribel hadn't been here for long, the place hadn't taken on her style, her character.

The room held a bed, a chair, a small dresser, and a closet. Maribel had a bag leaning against the closet door, propping it closed. Good chance she had a knife under the pillow, for protection, maybe a revolver in the bag if things went really poorly.

Maribel lounged on the bed, splayed out in an awkward imitation of a come-hither look. The room hadn't fit her, and she didn't fit it. She patted the simple yellow cotton sheets of the bed, saying, "Why don't you take a seat, let me get those boots off of you."

Roman kept an eye on the closet as he joined her. Maribel slipped off of the bed and kneeled to pull off his boots, which had been worn to as close a comfortable fit as they would ever be, still pinching at the heel.

"How long you been in town, Ms. Maribel?"

"Not too long. A month or so." Maribel set one boot aside. Roman stretched his foot, feeling the grains of sand roll against his toes. Oh, the shower he would take after the mission.

"Why here? Why not head all the way to the coast, San Francisco or the like?" he asked, trying to lure her out to get more information. Mallery figured something was up with the Mendoza brothers, but she hadn't been certain, at least that's what her notes said. Comparing Maribel to the feeds Mallery had sent back to HQ, the girl was almost definitely Juan's kin.

He'd bet good money Maribel was connected to the story, but he didn't know how aggressive to play the scene. But he was certain that he wasn't about to jump in bed with a teenager.

The girl struggled with the other boot, slipping it back and forth to shimmy it off of his heel.

"Oh, you know. Big city dreams turn out to be more expensive than you think. One delay and suddenly the money you had to get to the coast only gets you as far as Nowhere, Colorado, and you have to learn to make do."

"You came out West all on your own?"

Maribel finally got the other boot off, and set it beside the first.

"Yes, sir," she said. Maribel paused, no more boots to

fixate on. The next logical piece of undressing would be his shirt or pants, a substantial step up in intimacy.

She wavered in place and steadied herself on the bed frame.

"Miss?" he asked.

The girl raised a hand to bid him wait. She took several long breaths. But her breathing wasn't strained.

If he was a gambling man, and on worlds like this he was, she was faking it. But to what end?

"I'm not feeling so well, Mister Roman. If'n you don't mind, I think it'd be best if I ask Miss Sarah to send up someone else to look after you while I take a sit-down."

"I didn't ask for the other girls, Maribel. I asked for you."

Maribel stopped, body freezing. But not out of fear. More like she was weighing her options.

Roman scooted back on the bed, giving her space. "I'm going to make a guess, and if I'm wrong, I'll leave and you'll get your money, no fuss. But if I'm right, hear me out."

Maribel's hand slid across the bed, probably toward a knife or a holdout pistol.

Roman moved slow, raising his hands. "I'm not here to hurt you. But I'm guessing that your last name is Mendoza, and you had two brothers, Frank and Juan, until Matt Williamson and his gang killed one and scared the other one off."

He watched Maribel's eyes, already knowing the answer. "So am I right?"

"What do you want with me, then?" her words came out half-question, half-accusation.

"I'm mighty sorry about your brother. My friends and I, we're here to stop the Williamsons, but we need Frank's help. So can you tell us where he is?"

"Oh, I wish I knew. He ran off from that fight, and I ain't seen him since. Miss Sarah said she'd shut me up tight when the Williamsons come 'round again, make sure they didn't know he still had kin in town."

Still dissembling, then. Roman sighed. "It's a shame. Would have been awful handy to meet the only man to survive a showdown with the Williamsons."

Roman let the words hang in the air, tuning his ears. He heard the creaking of wood in the hall.

Story worlds had a way of bending to your plans, as long as you set your intentions to match the tale types. What he needed right now was for Frank Mendoza to come and check on his sister.

And that was it. "But how could he have abandoned his little sister, with those bloodthirsty men sworn to come back for another try at the town? I mean, your brother's no coward, is he?"

Wood creaked again. Maribel stole a look to the door.

"I couldn't say, mister. Now why don't you lay back, and I'll get someone up here to help you forget all about those Williamsons."

Instead, Roman shot to his feet and pulled the door open, revealing Frank Mendoza, wearing a stain-worn apron.

Frank reached to his belt and came away with a revolver, flour-covered hand shaking. Roman stood perfectly still, not wanting to give Frank any more reason to shoot, having already startled the man.

"Frank Mendoza, I presume."

Frank shook in place. "We don't want no trouble, mister. So you best go on mosey yourself downstairs and forget about both of us." It was far harder to take Frank's threat seriously when his hand was shaking like he was in an earthquake. The gun was plenty dangerous, assuming it was loaded. But without control, that pistol was more hazard than weapon.

"How about you put that gun down, Frank," Roman said, trying to make his voice as calming as possible. "Shaking like that, you're more likely to hurt Maribel than me."

"This fella and his friends are going after the Williamsons." Maribel turned to Roman. "You gonna give us all the bounty on the Williamsons if he helps you get rid of them?"

Much better. "Of course. My friends and I, we heard about the Williamsons, and we mean to help you drive them off. Get justice for poor Juan and your other friends. But if we're gonna win this fight, we need you, Frank. You're the only one who has faced the Williamsons and survived."

Roman smiled, trying to warm up the situation. He didn't have the charm of Mallery or Shirin, but he'd been in scrapes like this before, sweet-talking at the business end of a barrel. He could just snatch the gun from the young man, but with Frank's finger already on the trigger, it was a risky play. "We drive them off, then my friends and I will get you and Maribel the next train to San Francisco, with some extra money besides. Plus whatever we recover from the bandits."

Frank was still shaking, but less so. Terror had given way to confusion, and Roman saw a flicker of hope in the young man's eyes.

And a flicker was all they needed to plant the seed of heroism.

Maribel crossed to her brother and pushed his hand down, lowering the gun. They talked in whispers, too low for Roman to hear anything other than that it was in Spanish.

The gun away, Maribel turned. "Why don't you bring your friends up here to talk, Roman?"

———————

Leah came in to fetch Miss Sarah, and once they'd explained, the madam gave the nod. The three of them went up discreetly over the next ten minutes to avoid suspicion. Well, any more than they already got as outsiders.

The group sat and stood in the room, Maribel sitting with her brother on the bed. Frank was jittery. Leah imagined if she'd walked away from a gunfight only twenty-four hours ago, she'd be jittery, too.

King introduced the team. "I'm King. You've met Roman. This is Lee, and Atlas Jane." Even King saying her cover reminded Leah of how strange it was to look down and see a stranger's body. She remembered to adjust her stance, switching from a cocked hip to leaning back against the wall, arms crossed.

Think dudely thoughts.

King continued. "I'm a State Marshal, and these are my deputies. Governor sent us over in a hurry after he heard what the Williamson gang did. And I don't cotton to bullies."

King pointed at Frank. "We'd like to help you with the Williamsons. And we've got a plan that will see them run off or bleeding on the street. But we need you for this fight."

"Your sheriff died in the shootout, and the deputy, too?" Shirin asked like she didn't know the answer. A fine interviewing skill. It was also a stand-up skill.

"Yep. Both of 'em," Frank said.

King steepled his hands, a chess master with words for his playing pieces. Dude was scary in action. "That means the town needs a new sheriff. Who could do the job?"

Frank looked to Maribel. "There ain't many gunslingers around. Miss Sarah says the town hasn't had trouble for a few years. Most folks ride right on by to the bigger towns, or hit the train coming out of Sandborne."

"That the truth, then?" King said. "In that case, I think we've got our new sheriff right here. The only man to face the Williamsons and live."

Frank froze like a deer in the headlights back home, refusing to move even as Leah's father yelled at it and waved it off the road.

King read the room, then turned back to Frank and Maribel. "Here's the offer. You help us take out the bandits, we get you set up as the new sheriff, or we get you train tickets to the coast. Either way, you get a purse to look after your sister and get your brother a proper burial."

Frank looked to his sister then down to his shaking hands.

"I . . . I'll try. But I can't promise nothing, Mr. King. I ain't no hero."

"You became a hero the moment you stepped up to face the Williamson gang the first time," King said. "What we're going to do now is make you a gunslinger. With training and my team at your back, we'll put Matt Williamson in the ground, restore peace in this town, and get you and your sister on your way to the coast."

King offered a hand. "Do we have a deal?"

Frank met King's hand, twitching from head to toe. "Deal."

"Excellent. We've got a few hours of sunlight. Meet me behind the saloon in five minutes." King nodded to Roman, then walked out of the room.

Four

Y'all are pullin', not squeezing

SQUINTING, LEAH LOOKED DOWN the sight of the heavy revolver at the tin cans and bottles that King and Roman had set up along the fence at the edge of the saloon property. A small hill in the background served as the backdrop, keeping their misses from endangering the neighbors.

"Both eyes open. Squinting kills your depth perception," said Roman from behind.

Leah opened her eyes, refocused, and pulled the trigger.

The gun kicked in her hands like a cat in 2 a.m. freakout mode, roared like a cannon shot, and yet her bullet smacked into the hill, at least a yard off-target.

Beside her, poor Frank was doing even worse. He held the revolver in both hands, his body recoiling from the gun, head turned away. Almost everything Leah knew about guns before that day came from watching TV, and even she knew Frank was holding it wrong.

"Grip, Frank. Let's start again." Roman stepped up beside the timid gunslinger, keeping a wary eye on the muzzle of the revolver. He put a steady hand on Frank's wrist, then took the gun and wrapped the scared young man's right hand around the grip, setting his finger along the stock.

If she didn't know better, Leah would have guessed that Frank was playing up the awkward to make "Lee" feel more comfortable. But that wasn't the way of it, and his twitchiness mostly made her more nervous. Nothing like your neighbor on the shooting range being as shaky as a jackhammer to tank any semblance of calm and focus.

Leah squeezed off a few more shots, going wide to the left, then to the right. She aimed again and put a bullet straight into the post . . . six inches below the can.

She adjusted again and fired, winging the can, which wobbled and then dropped off of the post.

Leah whooped.

Frank despaired. "He's already got it. I got shooting lessons from my pop and I ain't never hit nothing 'cept nothing. Are you sure I have to shoot to take the Williamsons out? Couldn't I just convince them to leave the town alone or something?"

"Silver-tonguing ain't going to get justice for your brother, Frank," King said. "You're the hero this town needs. You stand up to the Williamsons again, people here will notice. And you stare a man down, a man who tried to kill you and failed, you've got something."

"I know what I'll have. Shame. Shame I couldn't save my brother."

"The dead don't hold nothing over you, Frank. There will be time to bury Juan, but if you don't learn how to shoot, you'll be running your whole life. Someone has to protect your family."

Frank looked to Maribel, who leaned against the back of the saloon, pointedly not watching the scene. It looked like Maribel was even less interested in guns than her brother, but wanted to show her support.

"Okay, now try again," Roman said.

A half hour and another fifty bullets later, Leah had hit ten targets, Frank had hit one. Accidentally. Ten feet from the target he was aiming at.

"Okay, that'll have to do for today," King said. "Frank, why don't you and I have a talk about breathing and focus. My years as Marshal taught me more than a few things about how men's minds work, and I reckon your problem is that you're your own worst enemy. Let's see if we can't get your mind and your body on the same side, okay?"

Frank nodded, eager to hand the gun back to Roman.

"Roman, you keep working with Lee," King said.

Leah shook out her wrist as the two men headed back inside, Maribel joining them after one parting look at Leah.

Either something in her grip was off, or guns really hurt to hold and fire.

"Can you show me that grip again? I think I'm doing something wrong," Leah said.

"No problem. Let's start from the beginning, with your stance."

Leah adjusted her footing, going for the square stance she'd been taught all of an hour ago. "So, how did you get into this crazy business?"

"Try this." Roman pushed her right leg out, widening her stance. "I did a little bit of this, little bit of that, traveled in Africa and the Middle East, and decided I wanted to get out of the corporate violence business. I was looking for a way out, and King found me."

"Seems like he's got a neat little talent for that. Finding people."

"That what happened with you, then? Getting tired of comedy?" Roman took the gun and placed it back in her hands, wrapping her right around the grip, her left on her right. "Finger off the trigger until you're ready to fire.

Make a strong frame with your hands, arms, and shoulders. Connect everything through the torso to the feet, or the recoil will spoil your aim."

Leah adjusted, trying to figure out what it felt like to connect the hands, arms, torso, and feet with this weapon. She'd learned just enough about guns to know she didn't like them. "Tired of comedy, no. Tired of receptionisting, yes. You were what? Security? Private military contractor?"

"Something like that. It was the best way out of a bad situation. Until King came along and showed me a better way." Roman pointed to the fence. "When you're ready to fire, sight down the barrel, center your target, place your finger on the trigger, and squeeze."

"And when was that?" Leah fired, hitting the fence beneath the can. Better than missing the target zone entirely.

"Almost ten years ago," Roman said. "You're flinching before you fire, anticipating the recoil. Stay steady, exhale as you squeeze the trigger."

"And you like it?" Leah took a long breath, recentered on the target, checked her stance and grip, and exhaled, squeezing the trigger.

And the can went flying. Mostly sideways, a glancing blow, but she'd hit. "Yes!" she said, throwing both hands up in the air.

"Careful," Roman said in a level voice, hands out and calming.

"Ah, yeah," Leah said, remembering the lethal weapon she was cheering with, bringing the gun back down to a ready position.

"Better. And yes, I love it. Best job I've ever had. The cause is good, the pay is better, and life is better when I'm not on-mission. Out in the field, kicking around in a F.O.B., there's a lot of down time, but unless you're back home, there's always that niggling sliver of fear, that need to be always ready, the idea that even when you're shirtless and gambling while the guy next to you is dreaming up some stupid prank to pull on his buddy, some a-hole could be about to drop a bomb on you."

"Yeah, not a lot of bombing going on in southern Maryland." Leah stopped herself. "Right? The genre worlds can't, like, send bombs over from War Movie world to take us out?"

"Line up another shot," Roman said. Leah detected a chuckle under his instructor seriousness, and marked herself a point in the comedy success column.

Leah did her best to repeat the ritual Roman had given her, taking aim at the next can. This shot went wide, but barely.

"Close. Go ahead and move over so you've got the straight shot headed uphill," Roman said. "And no, the other worlds don't know that we even exist. Science division says things would get really bad if they did."

"Yeah," Leah said. "Imagine a whole world suddenly realizing they're in the Matrix all at once."

"No one likes to realize they're not in on the joke. These worlds make sense internally, and even when stories break down, they carry on without any outside interference. If we did more than small fixes, or if the worlds knew what else was out there . . ." Roman stopped, as if trying to remember. "I think the phrase Preeti used was 'Absolute ontological deterioration,' which sounds like a bad time."

"No one gets to see behind the curtain. Got it." Leah squared off and fired, hitting the can and sending it flying back.

"Dead on. Nicely done. When you get out of your way, look what happens?" he said, walking over to retrieve the can. Leah lowered the gun, remembering the muzzle discipline that had started the lecture, along with trigger discipline and ten minutes of other safety discussions. Roman plucked the can up and turned it to show Leah a hole straight through the middle.

"Story of my life."

"Getting out of your own way, or a bullet through the heart?" Roman asked, his instructor's demeanor cracking.

"That's an affirmative to both, good sir," Leah said.

"Fair enough. Now, let's try without moving to recenter."

———

King sat Frank down on the bed in the room he shared with his sister. King remained standing.

"You and your brother stood up to the Williamson gang in the first place. That means you've got some courage already. The fact that you ran means that you have fear. Courage and fear go hand in hand, like a horse and rider. Courage is knowing a bronco is bucking and deciding to jump on its back anyway, knowing you may get thrown. So what we need now is to figure out how to get you back on the horse, calm your nerves, until you can prove to yourself that you can ride, that you can conquer your fear. That clear?"

Frank nodded. "Yes, sir."

"Why did you and your brother step up? What were you thinking when you said yes, when you strapped on that gun belt and went out into the noonday sun to face those bandits?"

"My brother, he volunteered first. And I . . . I couldn't let him go alone."

"Loyalty, then. You wanted to protect your brother."

"Yes, sir."

"Just like you want to protect your sister."

Frank flexed his hands, looking at the floor. "Yes, sir."

"You won't have to do this alone, Frank. My team, we've solved problems like this before. But if some outsider solves a town's problem for them, what happens? Solving people's problems for them never made them more capable of anything."

King knelt down to speak to Frank, eye to eye, ignoring the popping in his knees and the accompanying pain. "What I want is to help you save this town. For folks to be able to remember Frank Mendoza as the man who avenged his brother's death, who ran the Williamson gang out of town with the help of some Marshals. You haven't lived here long, but this town claims you as their own, that much is clear."

"Well, we've tried to make friends, since our money ran out. Miss Sarah's been mighty generous, putting us up here in the saloon."

"And you can repay that generosity by believing in yourself."

King stood slowly, not interested in spending his aging knees on a pep talk when there was a gunfight on the horizon. Frank was a tricky case. Most heroes-in-waiting just took the smallest push out of the door to get started on the path.

But this was a breach, and if his brother was meant to be the hero, that'd explain some of the hesitation. But they had the time they had, he just needed to solve the puzzle of Frank. "Think back to a time when you were perfectly calm, when you stood up and licked whatever the problem was."

Again, Frank looked at his hands and the floor below.

"There has to be something. Some time in your life—"

Frank cut in. "It's stupid."

"I'm sure it's not. Everyone's life is their own, Frank. Your triumphs are still triumphs."

"I was cooking. It was a dinner party for my cousin's engagement. The milk went sour, so I had to go and get more, and I forgot about my tortillas, so they burnt and I had to start over. But instead of getting frustrated and giving up, I started over. And it got done, and it was delicious, and the dinner was perfect. After that . . ."

King cut Frank off, sensing the dip in Frank's mood. He had to keep the boy focused on the positive.

"That. That right there. Why did you start over without wallowing?"

"I knew it had to get done, and worrying weren't going to help no one."

King stopped, pointing a finger. He tapped Frank on the shoulder. "That's how you need to think. The

Williamson gang needs to be stopped. Worrying and panicking won't help nobody. We can teach you how to shoot, how to move in a fight, find and use cover. You just have to get back on that horse, see?"

"I was never good at riding, Mr. King. Might be better for you to find another way of talking 'bout this."

It'd been a while since King'd had a hero quite this reluctant. But this wasn't the first time a story breach had gone weird. HQ was getting troubling reports from the other bases, on top of the missions he and the Mid-Atlantic teams had been working. Something was rippling across the worlds. These breaches were different. Maybe some kind of dimensional El Niño or the like, a system of incongruities in the breaches. Yet another topic for his next report to the High Council.

King went to the door.

"Here's a thought. Why don't we get a head start on dinner, and you show me what you can do. If I see you in your element, maybe I can get an idea of how to make gunfighting make sense, seem less terrifying. And if we don't, then we still have dinner for everyone. Seems reasonable, don't you think?"

Frank stood, more light in his face than he'd seen since he met the boy. "Yes, sir. Everyone needs to eat, and being on the frontier is no excuse for eating poorly."

King stepped aside, leaving room for Frank. "In that

case, after you."

———————

Leah had seen firsthand that Frank Mendoza was a public menace with a revolver, but it turned out he was a saint with a saucepan. Which, for a Western, was pretty odd.

Miss Sarah arranged for the team and the Mendozas to take dinner in the kitchen alone, so Frank could come down without being seen in public. The six of them crowded around a table, making stutter-stop attempts toward conversation that happened with people you'd met, especially in groups.

Frank was as calm and confident in the kitchen as he was clammy and shaky on the shooting range. Put him in an apron and set a stove and some pots in front of him and he was The Man With No Name. No wasted motion, no hesitation. He poured water and worked a spoon with precision and grace, happily explaining every step.

Frank had some core of confidence to work from, so getting him to step up would be a matter of connecting that core confidence he had with cooking to shooting.

Or maybe coming up with some crazy crossover Iron Chef kind of way to make cooking into fighting. Have him go into battle with a meat tenderizer and paring knife.

Still, as funny as that image was, it was odd. In Leah's memory of Westerns, most of the reluctant heroes were farm hands or would-be ranchers. They wanted to be gunslingers, but didn't believe in themselves. Frank definitely didn't believe in himself, but in any other story, he'd be a supporting character. But King and the team seemed pretty confident that this was their hero. Something about the story just didn't fit. Maybe that was because the world had gone so off-kilter.

Everyone was feeling one another out—Maribel and Frank played it close to the chest, King and the Genrenauts were trying to steer conversation away from themselves as best as they could, presumably along their Prime Directive-y agenda to tread lightly. Leah was mostly content to watch King and the Genrenauts work, like having a movie unfold right in front of your eyes, one where half the cast knew they were in a story, and the other half didn't. *Cabin in the Woods* without the blood sacrifice.

Frank chatted up a storm. "You should have seen poor Juan with that dog, they looked like they'd been put through the wash and left out to dry."

Shirin and Roman played the role of the easy audience, and Leah remembered herself enough to smile along. The weirdness of the situation, the onion-tastic meta was hitting hard. The wrongness of the story niggled at her mind, like a chunk of popcorn that she couldn't quite pick out with her tongue. The more she tried to relax and observe, the more the wrongness stood out to her.

Food, however, made sense. Leah held her plate out for another serving of cornbread. Cooking and serving, Frank was almost a whole other person, completely in his element, not a shaking hand to be seen. But did that mean he could stand up to the bandits?

Frank dished out food to the entire Genrenauts team, as well as filling plates for saloon staff and customers. All while keeping up his end of a conversation about the Mendozas' life before they'd come out West.

"Why leave Texas?" Shirin asked.

Frank shared a look with his sister, who had changed out of the frippery and was wearing a simple floral dress.

Maribel picked up the conversational thread. "Well, you see Frank here wants to open a restaurant, but there weren't no way he could do it in Wichita Falls, Texas. He won't settle for anything less than the fanciest of clientele, with the prices to match. So we saved up as much as we could, sold most everything we owned aside from Frank's pots, Juan's guns, and my books, and bought ourselves tickets as far west as we could manage. That got us here. We'd only meant to stay long enough to buy the tickets to San Francisco."

"I know I could get a job in any restaurant out there, if they would only give me a chance," Frank added.

Maribel set her dish in the sink and kissed Frank on the cheek. She said something in Spanish, then walked out the back door.

Leah wiped her mouth with a napkin and stood, following Maribel on a hunch she didn't know she'd had until she was halfway to the door.

But King and company had talked about following your instincts and everything, so she went with it.

Winds drew sand into swirls, catching the red-pink light of the setting sun. The same wind tickled at the hem of Maribel's dress. The woman leaned against a wooden pillar of the back porch, looking west to the sunset.

"Everything alright?" Leah asked, stepping into Maribel's field of vision. The woman bristled for a moment, then relaxed.

"I'm fine. Just like watching the sunset, is all. It's the same sun, no matter where you go, but it seems a little brighter here, the moon a little closer. Or maybe this town's really that much smaller."

"I thought you came from a small town?"

"Small, but not tiny. This here's a stopover town, perfectly fine aside from the bandits, but nowhere for us to put down roots. Especially after . . ."

"I bet. I imagine if I were in your shoes, I couldn't put

this town in my"—Leah caught herself before using totally out-of-genre language—"dust fast enough."

"Turns out it's not easy to just up and make money when you're away from home. Ms. Sarah's been right kind to us, and she treats Frank better than any fancy San Francisco restaurant would, I reckon."

"And how are you dealing with, I mean, having to . . . ?" Leah asked.

"I ain't had to take no customers, if'n that's what you're asking about. And I don't intend to start, if you're asking."

Leah wondered if the PPM would hide a blush. She focused on the story, trying to hold the structure in her mind, the moving parts that were Maribel and Frank and the bandits. But how did it all fit together? Her gut told her Maribel would play a bigger role in this story. She stood out too much to be just the doting sister.

"I made a deal with Ms. Sarah," Maribel continued. "She needed to look like she had more girls on her roster, so I dress the part but if someone picks me, I fake like I'm sick. I was faking a fainting spell when your friend started in about the Williamsons."

"Wouldn't people notice eventually?" *There's more to her. But what?* Leah thought, racking her brain for the right angle.

She shrugged. "Eventually. Ms. Sarah looked to be

getting a bit nervous, but she didn't want to lose Frank's cooking. And the other girls are plenty nice to me, especially since I ain't taking their money. And on account of me looking out for their little ones while they work."

"That's . . . a lot simpler, I guess. So what are you going to do when you get out to the coast?"

Maribel looked out to the sunset, like she was looking all the way to the coast, to her future. "Keep Frank out of trouble, run the parts of the restaurant he can't be bothered with, assuming he can get the money together to give it a shot. Frank talks big, but he's not the one for follow-through."

Ding ding ding. That's it. "But you are?" Leah said.

Maribel closed her eyes, wrapping an arm around the pillar. "'Fraid so."

"How's that?"

Maribel looked up at the darkening sky, clouds stretched thin in staggered lines.

Leah could swear she was right on the edge of something. King was agitated about Frank not stepping up, and something about Maribel couldn't help but stand out—she wasn't your average Western leading lady. She wasn't a schoolmarm, wasn't a prostitute. There had to be some "supportive sister" characters in the genre somewhere, but all of the narrative math added up to tell Leah that there was more going on here.

Leah repeated her question. "What do you mean by that, Maribel?"

It was probably her mind playing tricks on her, but Leah thought she could see frayed edges at the end of Maribel's elbows and at her cheek. Just for a second, like a shadow passing overhead. But the feeling stuck once the visual irregularity faded. Leah already knew Maribel's story was off, so what was this telling her?

"Is there something we should know, Maribel?"

"Shit." Maribel looked Leah straight on, her eyes moist. Her instincts said to lean on the woman, to push a bit harder. Something would come of it. "If Frank goes out with your boss, the Marshal, he's going to get himself killed, isn't he?"

"I don't know," Leah said. "The others in my posse, they've been doing this for a while. But they need Frank for their plan to work. If he steps up and then freezes again, he's going to die, and maybe the rest of us with him."

Maribel wiped the almost-tears from her eyes and stood up straight, taller than Leah had thought she really was.

"I love him like the sunset, but Frank's no gunslinger. Never was, never will be. Juan wanted to be, but he never had the gift."

"But you did?" Leah asked, connecting the dots. *They*

said trust your instinct. *Hope it doesn't blow up in my face.*

Maribel sighed.

Leah knew that sigh. That was the sigh of regret. It was the sigh she'd used when she questioned moving out to Baltimore, questioned her desire to do stand-up. It came up a lot, actually. "I had the skill," Maribel said. "Just not the judgment."

"How's that?"

"Why don't we go back inside. I don't have it in me to tell this story more than once," Maribel said, then without another word, walked back inside.

Leah turned on her heels and followed. *And cue the revelation scene.*

———

Leah watched as Maribel walked up to the table and looked King in the eyes.

"Y'all need to know something. My brother's a lot of things. He's kind, he's funny, and he's the best hand in the kitchen I ever met. But he's no hero. You can't take Frank out there to face those men. I ain't going to stand by and watch another brother get gunned down."

"Maribel, we don't have to tell . . ." Frank said.

"I have to, Frank. We been running for too long."

Maribel squeezed her brother's hand. "He's no

fighter, Mr. King. He and Juan joined that posse so I wouldn't have to."

"Explain," King said, fingers steepled, expression flat.

"Back home, I got into a whole passel of trouble. We lived in Wichita Falls, you see, home of Kid Cole. He was always strutting about town like he owned the place. He took a shining to my friend Sue-Anne, shot dead three other men who came calling on her. But Sue-Anne, she didn't want nothing to do with Cole.

"So one morning, when he was standing on Sue-Anne's porch again yellin' at her to get out there and talk to him, I took Juan's gun and went off to pick a fight. Put two in the air before he could shoot once. Shot him dead, I did. But the other bullet went wide."

Maribel closed her eyes, looked down to her hands. "It ricocheted off a pole behind Kid Cole and hit Sue-Anne through the window. Struck her dead before she hit the ground. So there I was with two deaths on my hands and more guilt than justice."

Frank squeezed Maribel's hand as she sniffed back tears.

"Then it got worse. I knew Kid Cole had rich family, but no one told me he was the nephew of a circuit judge."

"We had to get away from the judge," Frank said. "So we packed up and left."

"Figured if I dressed up all feminine-like, we could lie

low and make it to the coast, far out of the judge's jurisdiction."

"But you can't," Leah said. "Someone needs to stand up to the Williamsons. It should be you."

"Did you see the Williamsons?" King asked Maribel.

Another nod.

"How bad are they?" Shirin asked.

"One-on-one, I could do for Matt. But there's five of them. And after Sue-Anne, I swore I wouldn't touch another gun 'til the day I die."

"We're talking about your brother's killers," Leah said.

"And I want them dead as surely as you do. But if I pick that gun up, I'm saying that what I did to Sue-Anne didn't matter."

"The way I hear it, you took up the gun to do something she couldn't do for herself," Shirin said. "Your brother can't take up the gun, but you can. Let us help you put your brother's spirit to rest, and you might find that the ghost of Sue-Anne is put to rest, too."

"Here's what we'll do, then," King said. "You get to square off with Matt and the gang when they come back, say your piece, and then we put the lot of them in the dirt. And when it's done, you and Frank get the bounty on the Williamson gang. That should get you to the coast with enough left over to get you started on that restaurant."

King opened his hands, his body language open, approachable. "What happened to Sue-Anne—that was Cole's doin', not yours. Would Sue-Anne want you to just stand by, knowing you could have done something to help this town? A town that can't save itself? You made a terrible mistake and you're living with it. But you're never going to make one like that again, are you? You're going to be better."

And that was why he was the boss.

Frank squeezed his sister's hands. "Don't do it. We can lie low, put the money together somehow, get out of here once things blow over."

Maribel wrapped her shaking brother up in her arms, hands running through his hair. She looked King dead in the eyes. "I ain't going to leave this town until I've put those men what killed my brother in pine boxes."

Leah said, "You got yourself a hero. Now don't make me regret it."

Roman joined in, "You already know how to shoot. And you know what you're fighting for. But if you want to kick the dust off, I reckon we've got about a half-hour of light left between twilight and the torches."

"That's a fine excuse to get out of doing the dishes," Frank added.

King scooted out his chair and stood. "Lee and I will handle those."

The dinner party broke up, each to their next task.

Leah shot King a look, hoping to mean "Look at that! I did something!"

His response was hard to read. Guy was made of poker face. But Leah knew she'd done good. She could boast later.

———————

After sunset, the group reassembled in the saloon, again claiming the corner booth. Maribel changed and joined them, far more comfortable in spats and a collared shirt than in a working girl's frills and lace. Frank stayed upstairs, wanting no part in Maribel getting herself killed, so he said.

Shirin rolled out a piece of paper and took charcoal to it, drawing out a map of the town.

"Where'd they come in from, last time?" Shirin asked.

Maribel tapped the paper on the east end of the street. "They came in this way. The Douglas ranch saw them first, sent Joey to ride into town and warn folks. Frank, Juan, and the sheriff's posse met them here," she said, pointing to the bank.

"Got it," Shirin said. "In that case, our best spots are here, on the roof of the bank, the church bell tower here, and the roof of the saloon."

"Ain't no way onto the roof of the saloon unless you got a ladder," Maribel said.

"We'll find one," Shirin said. "If not, Roman here's a fair climber." Roman nodded, showing the hint of a grin.

"Or we make it simple. Shirin can set up in the bell tower with the long rifle, the rest of us will be on the ground with you," King said to Maribel.

The woman considered the map. "Five of us, five of them. The sheriff winged at least one of 'em last time, so we've got that on them, too," Maribel said. "You keep the others busy, and I'll do for Matt Williamson just fine."

"We'll have your back," King said.

"Why not set up an ambush?" Leah asked. "Take them out as they're coming in?"

"I want to see the light go out of those bastards what killed Juan," Maribel said.

King didn't challenge her. Leah filed the question away for later.

Five

High Eleven-Thirty-Ish

LEAH WOKE TO oppressively loud knocking on the door. She fumbled about the room in a haze. Dimensional jet lag had kept her up for hours, and when she did sleep, it was poorly.

"Yeah, yeah," she said, waving at the door, holding her other hand up to her eyes to block out the morning sun that cut through the window.

Ms. Sarah and the saloon had put the team up for the night. Her room was small and sparse, but really all she needed was a place to pass out. Though in creaky retrospect, maybe a nicer bed would have helped.

The washing facilities made her miss camping trips with the family, which was saying something. After her cold sponge bath, she made her way down to the kitchen. Frank manned the stove, grilling and frying and looking far more comfortable wearing an apron than she wagered he would wearing a bandolier.

The rest of the team was already assembled, looking

like the Western version of firefighters sitting and waiting for the call. King had shaved, Roman had not.

Shirin pulled up a chair. "Good morning, kiddo. Coffee?"

"Please yes now," Leah said, her brain not done spooling up. She'd taken exactly one 8 a.m. class in college, a chem lab the school didn't offer any other time. If it'd been at eleven, she was sure she'd have gotten an A. Instead, she swallowed her C+ and moved on, glad that the science requirements for a theater degree were minimal.

Shirin handed her a tin cup of coffee. She didn't bother sniffing, and went straight to pouring the java down her gullet. It was thick, and fairly pungent, but it did the job of ripping off a layer of her fatigue like it was a waxing. Painful, but over in a moment.

Maribel walked into the room, holding her own tin of coffee. In pants and without a bustier, she moved like a ranging big cat. Ready to pounce in a moment.

"Today's the day, then," Maribel said. "Ms. Sarah's got the word out that we'll be waiting for the Williamsons. I figure they'll show by noon. Everything set on your end?"

King set down his coffee. "All ready. Atlas Jane's got enough shells to take on an army."

Maribel leaned in, and Leah did her best at concealing her eavesdropping. Luckily, Leah was excellent at being nosy.

"Anything happens to me, you get my brother out of town. Get him somewhere so he can be the fancy chef he was supposed to be."

"It'll be done," King said. "But don't worry. I've been at this for a very long time, as have my posse." King raised his voice back to normal conversational levels. "Aside from Lee here. He's new, and we haven't decided if he's going to run off or if he'll be running circles around me within a year. He's already a champion eavesdropper."

Leah's cheeks went hot. She leaned back in her chair, facing King. "Can you blame me? If I'm going to walk into a firefight, I'd like to know what I'm getting into."

"That's fair," Maribel said. "Walking into a fight blind is a great way to end up with a permanent view of the inside of a pine box."

Roman raised his cup to toast.

"Okay, grub's up!" Frank said, moving with enthusiastic precision, doling out sausage, eggs, and hash from his skillet. "Sorry I can't do anything more—limited materials and all. I picked up a gumbo recipe back home before we left, and I've been dying to try it out." Frank stopped, a chill passing over him. "I mean, I wanted to try it. But the general store here doesn't get none of that sort of thing. I ain't seen a shrimp or saltwater fish in weeks."

"It's wonderful," Shirin said. "Thank you for the

breakfast."

"I just wish I could be of more use than frying up eggs. Maribel here's the real deal."

"When we get to the coast," Maribel said, "it's your picky palate and steady hands that'll be making us rich. I figure we can get to owning three restaurants by next winter, we play our cards right."

Leah saluted with her coffee tin. "That's what I like to hear. What will you call your restaurant, Frank?" she asked, hoping to distract the siblings from the coming danger. Hell, herself, too.

The cook moved between the stove and tables without pausing, his face bright.

"Oh, that's been the hardest part. I want to cook so many different styles of food, so it'd need to be something not so specific to one cuisine."

"What about The Globe Café?" Leah suggested.

Frank stopped and cocked his head to the side, then resumed serving. "The Globe Café. Not bad. Better than Maribel's idea."

Leah turned, expecting the answer.

Maribel shrugged. "I think Little Brother's Bistro is a great name."

"But I'm older than you," Frank said.

"You get to be the older brother when you make us our fortune. Until then . . ."

Frank slid hash and eggs onto Leah's plate. She raised a hand as he approached with the sausage. "I don't eat meat, sorry."

Vegetarianism was a thing then, right? She hoped that cover would play in Western World. Traditional Western heroes were always steak-and-eggs types.

Shirin elbowed Leah. Maybe she should have been "not very hungry" instead.

The older Genrenaut covered for her. "Lee here got the runs last time he had meat on the road."

"Ah, that's a shame," Frank said. "I promise, this meat's plenty fresh, and well-cooked."

Roman offered up his cleared plate. "I'll take the kid's share if he's too lily-livered."

Frank dished out the sausage to Roman and came back with more hash, which Leah accepted with her most gracious smile.

"Get your breakfast down quick," King said. "We need to get ourselves into place. Frank, maybe you could wrap up some of those sausages for us in case the Williamsons make us wait?"

"Sure thing. But they won't be as good when they're cold."

"I'd rather be on time with cold sausages than late and dead with a full stomach."

"Sign me up for death by full stomach," Roman said.

"In another forty years or so."

"You keep eating like that, your heart won't give you forty years." Shirin pointed to the plate full of second helping, slathered in grease.

"Yes, Mother," Roman said, making a face.

———

Shirin's earpieces had been tested, retested, and were in perfect working order. Leah had never seen a radio that small, not one that wasn't limited to Bluetooth networks. And they would be way outside Bluetooth range, especially with Shirin in the tower.

"Some places, we can get away with tech. Other worlds, we have to be inconspicuous," Shirin said, fitting Leah with the earbud in the washroom before heading out to their positions. "Just don't fiddle with it. The hat should do most of the work covering it up, and the PPM will do the rest."

"Why can't you take them out one by one as they come into town?" she asked Shirin on the comm.

"The more resonant the story, the stronger the patch. We need to play in-genre," Shirin said. "Sneaking around and assassinating bandits doesn't fit."

Shirin raised a finger of exception. "But when we go to Spy world, you and I can sneak around and assassinate to your heart's content."

"Next time we come here, can I skip the giant-sized hat?"

"Oh, honey, there are things you get to complain about, and the wardrobe is not one of them. This is what every new team member has to go through. Even King and me, though that was ages ago."

"You two have been at this for a long time, haven't you?" Leah asked.

"That we have. Best job I've ever had. Not every mission is as scary as this, though. A lot of the worlds aren't violent. Romance world is especially fun. It's all musicals and meet-cutes and schmoopiness."

"Note to self: ask for the rom-com beat," Leah said.

Shirin held Leah gently by the shoulders. "Good luck with that—Mallery has that niche locked down hard. So for now, you watch our back and keep the Williamsons out of the bank."

———

Leah stood inside the front room of the Bank and Trust, ten feet wide and twice as deep. One teller and the manager were all that remained of the staff. And no customers had come by in the two hours she'd been standing by as they waited for the Williamsons.

The streets dried up about eleven, everyone rushing to get their errands done or take the last train out before the bandits came back. The train whistled its departure as townsfolk piled in to escape to the next town over or stay with friends. As far as she could tell, only a few dozen folk remained, hiding behind boarded-up doors and watching from second-story windows. Even if they drove the Williamsons off, this town might not recover.

Leah knocked on the window, catching Maribel's attention. Roman and King shot the breeze on the porch beside her, watching the street but playing casual.

"How's it look out there?" she asked.

"Still dead quiet. No one 'cept the horses, and most of them are gone, corralled off the main street. No one wants to be in the crossfire."

She would think about that, wouldn't she? "I imagine the horses appreciate that."

"They would if you could tear them away from their feed. Dumb things."

"Aw, I like horses."

"How much time you spent on 'em, Lee?"

"I like *looking* at horses," Leah said.

"Well, try living—"

Maribel was cut off by Shirin's voice in Leah's ear. "Five riders on the horizon. It's time."

Roman knocked three times on the horse post, the

signal that the Williamsons were coming.

"Here they come. Good luck." Leah looked back at the empty room, the terrified staff. There was still money in the vault, if not much. But the Williamson gang didn't know that. All they'd know was that there was a new posse between them and the silver.

Leah wanted to be able to help, but even with an afternoon's worth of training, she wasn't going to stare down a band of killers, gig or no gig. King hadn't asked her to put her life on the line, and she hadn't offered. She just hoped she wasn't going to stand by and watch them gunned down the way Mallery had watched her posse lose.

"Smoke 'em," Leah said as the posse squared off in the street.

———————

Roman stood at the ready as the Williamsons advanced.

King called the fight. "Roman, you take the woman on the right, I'll take the big guy on the left. Leave the ones in the middle for last. Shirin will cover us.

"Talk to them first," King added, "but if they draw, all bets are off."

Maribel snapped her holster open, ready to draw. "I'm no Marshal, and I don't need no excuse to put down the men what shot Juan."

A short man with a several-times broken nose and an unkempt beard climbed down from his horse. Four others joined him.

The first was a tall woman with a rifle. The short guy's taller brother held a shotgun, but the others had six-shooters on their belts. Roman trusted that Shirin could drop the shotgunner or rifleman as an opener, make things easier for the crew on the ground.

"Well lookey here. What do we have today?" the short man said with a Tennessee accent. That would be Matt Williamson. "A little girl playing dress-up in her brother's clothes. And she's found herself a posse."

King addressed the bandits. "You can lay down your arms and go to jail, or we can let our irons do the talking."

"Who the hell are you? The Governor actually waste another lawman on this piss-hole of a town?" Matt said.

"I'm Maribel Lucia Mendoza." Her hand hovered over her holster. She took a step forward, breaking ranks and not stopping.

"Maribel, wait," Roman said.

"Mendoza?" said Matt. "I killed a Mendoza a couple days ago. The one went down before he could fire, then his kin dropped his gun and ran to hide behind Miss Sarah's skirts. That don't make me inclined to be afraid of their kid sister, dress-up or no." He grinned wide, teeth stained and rotted.

"I ain't my brothers." Maribel drew so fast Roman only saw a blur. She fired, and the big guy to Matt's right dropped on his ass. Western Genre rules applied, with bullets causing knockback impossible outside a story world.

Maribel kept Matt and Tom Williamson in her sights as she spoke to the rest. "You best get back on your horse and keep riding if you don't want to end up being dragged out of the town in a pine box."

In response, the Williamson gang scattered, drawing to fire. Roman drew and the street was swallowed in clouds of dust and the thunder-crack of gunfire.

Tom Williamson fell facedown in the dirt. That'd be Shirin. Roman took a spot behind a watering trough, shooting at the woman with the rifle while Maribel charged Matt Williamson. Maribel winged Matt and put another round in the big guy.

The riflewoman bolted for the alley between the general store and the blacksmith.

"Keep them from getting away!" King shouted, firing after her.

Williamson fired on Maribel, who dashed right, heading across the street, firing suppressing but not dangerous shots back toward the bank.

"Aaah!" came Leah's voice on the comms.

"Stay down, Kid. We've got this," Roman said.

Shirin's voice crackled through the earpiece. "I've lost eyes on the riflewoman."

Roman took another shot, catching a bandit in the off-arm. This was nothing like shooting at the range. The guns were lower-quality, and the rising dust kicked up by the fight was obscuring everything.

"I'll get her," Roman said. "Drop masquerade protocols and end this?"

"Just keep on them!" King shouted over the din. Another shot rang out, clipping his gun arm. The team lead dropped to a knee, then crawled for cover.

With King down, Matt Williamson took the free path for the saloon. Maribel fired after him, but Williamson was a fast bugger. He was inside before she could fire a second time, and once he was off the street, she stopped. She wouldn't risk another bystander, not with the ghost of Sue-Anne haunting her.

Roman launched to his feet, sprinting down the street toward the general store. "I'm on the riflewoman. Someone go help Maribel with Matt."

"King's wounded," Shirin said. "He needs first aid."

"I'll do it! I can go around back," Leah said.

"Negative. Do not engage." King's voice was strained, but resolute.

"Gotta start pulling my weight some time, right?

Don't worry, I don't intend on getting myself killed for a lousy stand-up gig."

As he turned into the alley after the riflewoman, Roman saw Leah hightailing it across the street, holding her hat down with one hand, the other shaking by the holster.

"Go get 'em, Kid," Roman said.

Six

Improvisation

Leah kept her head low, running with her torso bent over her legs, the dust kicked up by bullets and shuffling proving enough concealment to make it across the street as the gunfire continued. She'd seen Maribel head into the saloon through the front door, following Williamson, so instead, she ran for the back door to cut him off from the kitchen.

"Pulling some daft heroics is not going to impress me, Ms. Tang," King said.

"I got this. I'm not going to try to take him on alone. All I need to do is find a way to help Maribel. She's the hero, right?" Leah grabbed the back corner of the building and caught herself to turn, not as gracefully as she'd like. She slowed as she reached the door, then tried to move as quietly as she could.

The door creaked as she stepped into the kitchen, where one of Ms. Sarah's girls sat drinking lemonade. She yelped when she saw "Lee." Leah put a finger to her mouth in the hopefully inter-dimensional sign for "Shush."

"Where?" she mouthed, pointing toward the main room. The working girl gave an exaggerated shrug.

Leah pressed herself up against the wall, inching toward the swinging door that led between the kitchen and the bar. She looked through the narrow band of glass into the main room. People cowered behind overturned tables, with Ollie the bartender hiding behind the bar, apparently not the type to keep a shotgun next to the rail liquor. More's the pity.

Maribel stood a step inside the swinging front doors, her gun out. Opposite her, Matt Williamson stood at the base of the stairs, holding his gun to Frank's head.

Dammit, Leah thought to herself, wishing Frank had stayed out of the way. But of course he'd have been watching as close as he could, with his sister putting her life on the line.

"Put down that gun, or you'll be fresh out of brothers," Matt said. Mirabel had tipped her hat, owned up to being a Mendoza, so what did Matt do, he went straight for Frank. The situation was as trope-y as they got. Family hostage, hero has to choose between getting the bad guy and saving their loved one.

Maribel spun her gun around, slowly, holding it by the sight and cylinder, no position to fire. "Just hold on, now. Don't nobody else need to get hurt today. My brother ain't even shot none of your crew, unlike me. Why don't we step outside and settle this, like I said."

"Little girl playing cowboy. You had enough yet? Put that gun down and I let your yeller brother leave town. You're fast, but not that fast," he said, pressing the barrel of his gun into Frank's temple. The chef shook from head to toe, wet eyes closed like he was shutting out the world with the hope that it'd go away.

Leah tried to work out a plan.

If she made noise to distract Matt, would Maribel have the time to fire?

Would she be able to hit without hurting Frank? Or would the noise just make Williamson shoot Frank?

Could she hit Williamson through the glass?

If she opened the door for a clear shot, would he notice?

There were too many variables, too many possibilities. They slammed at her from all sides like hail on a corrugated metal roof, her heart pounding in time.

She wasn't a hero, not yet. She was the Kid, the helper. And the helper usually ended up kidnapped and/or killed.

"Think, Leah, think."

But what if I'm not the Kid? she thought. *What if I'm the Rookie Sidekick?* She'd been the one to get Maribel to open up, to step up to join the cause. That could be the Kid or the Sidekick.

And in a finale, the Rookie Sidekick fought with whatever they could get their hands on. Their role was to give the hero the chance they needed to make the shot.

The back stairs. That was it. She turned and pointed to the girl, trying to use completely incorrect sign language to tell her to keep Williamson from coming into the kitchen. The girl shrugged again, apparently nonchalant about the gunfight in the room next door.

Leah grabbed the pitcher of lemonade right off the table and made for the work stairs beyond the kitchen, the set Frank had used to come and go out of sight. She walked the line between speed and stealth, making her way up, over, and then to the top of the L-shaped stairs that led down from the second floor to the main room.

Which put her above and behind Matt Williamson. Upstairs, all the doors were closed, unsurprisingly. Anyone who was getting busy had better things to do, or were at least smart enough to put a closed door between them and people with guns.

Leah stood at the top of the stairs and yelled, in her best Tough Miner voice. "I ain't paying!" She set the lemonade down, soft, at the top of the stairs.

In an exaggerated feminine voice—with a strong thread of Betty Boop—Leah shouted, "You rat! After two hours! Ms. Sarah, Ms. Sarah!"

Leah fired her gun at the thick side wall, no chance of hitting anyone or anything on a ricochet. And at the same time, she kicked the lemonade. The carafe shattered on the stairs, spilling and sloshing and making a marvelously distracting racket. Directly behind Matt Williamson.

Looking down to the first floor, she saw that her trick had done what it needed to. Williamson, confused, looked up and back. Leah waved a taunt, but before he could move, Frank dropped to the floor as a gunshot rang out.

Matt Williamson fell back onto the stairs, his revolver clattering to the ground beside him.

Lemonade spilled down the stairs, soaking the bandit's back as he went limp, red blooming on his chest.

Frank dashed away, and Maribel walked up on Williamson, kicking the gun out of the dying man's hands.

"That's a nice trick, there," Maribel said.

Leah stared at the body, her hand still shaking. He was dead. Because of her. He deserved it, but that was a dead body in front of her and he wasn't coming back. She sat, steadying herself on the railing to the stairs, the world closing in and zooming out at the same time.

"Status!" came King's voice, impatient and strained.

Leah breathed, words not yet coming. She took her eyes off of the body and turned away from Maribel. "Williamson's . . . dead," Leah said.

"What about the tall one?"

"She got away," Roman said. "She's got some serious hand-to-hand chops. Caught me by surprise."

Silence for a moment. That woman must have been something serious to give Roman the slip.

"The other bogies all down?" King asked.

"Nothing going outside," said Shirin.

"That's what I like to hear. Meet up in the saloon so we can debrief and denouement."

Leah wobbled to her feet and walked the other way, doing everything she could to put the image of Matt Williamson's body out of her mind. She knew it was coming, but to see death up close, to watch it . . . she wouldn't get that image out of her mind, probably ever.

And that's why Western heroes were defined by their grit.

Seven

Ritual and Reward

WITH THE BANDITS DEAD, tied up, or gone, the Genrenauts returned to the dinner table in the kitchen. Maribel had removed her hat, hair down but braided behind her back. Frank was cooking once again. The smell of beans and rice filled the kitchen, as well as the crackle of tortillas frying.

Leah tried to help tend to King's wounds, help preserve life to cancel out helping to end life just minutes ago, but the team leader waved her off. Roman bandaged the man's arm and put it in a sling, but he looked about as good as you could expect for a guy who had been shot.

Leah poured herself a drink and downed it in one peaty gulp. Her hand stopped shaking after a few minutes.

"So you always lose control of things like that?" Maribel asked with a smile. "I don't recall anything about distracting Williamson by enacting a stage show up on the second floor."

"No, that was all on the fly," King said. "And none too shabby, either. 'Cept for the fact that he was told not to go off and do something stupid like that."

"I'm just glad I came up with the idea between the back stairs and the second-floor landing."

"You made that up on the spot?" Frank asked, aghast.

"I was on the stage back home. I'm used to thinking on my feet."

"Looks like you picked your posse well, Marshal," Maribel said.

"I like to think so," King said. He leaned over, wincing, and pulled a bottle of far nicer liquor out of a bag. "Lee, get me three glasses."

Leah rose and retrieved glasses.

"Not those," Frank said as she pulled down the tin cups. "They have nice glass." The chef opened another cupboard and passed her three fine wine goblets.

Leah set the glasses down in front of the Genrenauts.

"Now get one for yourself," King said.

Frank grinned as he handed Leah another glass.

"Newbie or no, you're in our outfit, now," Roman said.

King poured a finger of amber-colored liquor into each glass. "We have a ritual on this team, whenever we complete a job. Victory without a celebration, well, that's like a story without a proper ending. Every story has its shape, and in this one, we found a hero, set things right, and broke in a new member of the posse." King raised his glass to Maribel, and to Leah, respectively.

"Should you be drinking if you got shot?" Leah asked.

"Hell, that just means he should drink more," Roman said.

King cleared his throat, taking control of the conversation again. "To another happy ending," King said, toasting. Leah raised her glass, and they clinked together in a happy mess of sound. Shirin gave Leah an affectionate squeeze on the shoulder, and Roman winked, leaning back as he drank.

Leah tossed back the drink as a shot before she realized that everyone else was sipping.

But as a testament to the alcoholic rigor of her college days, she did not do a spit-take when the peaty-as-a-barrow-wight's-butt liquor hit her tongue and nose.

She set the glass down hard, only gasping a bit.

"Did I forget to mention this was a sipping scotch?" King said.

"Tarnation!" Leah said, half-coughing, half-chuckling.

King leaned forward and poured another half shot into Leah's glass. "And to Maribel, the hero of the day. May the word of her deeds spread from the Mississippi straight to the coast. And may her brother's restaurant become the toast of the town."

Maribel toasted with her own cup, filled with a heavy portion of what Ollie had declared "the best whiskey in the house."

"What do you think the town will do now for a sheriff?" Frank asked.

King said, "Once we report back to the Governor, he'll send someone along soon enough. We heard a larger response was needed, and we were closer than any of the folks available."

"We'll be long gone by then," Frank said. "There was some . . . I mean, now that the Williamsons are gone . . ."

Maribel took over for Frank. "What my brother's trying to say is that I'm asking for the bounty we were promised. Matt, Tom, plus two more. Even those what your team brought down, like you offered."

"And as the Governor's representative, I'll make good on that promise." King reached into his bag again, pulling out a pouch the size of his fist. "You put your life on the line, so you ought to be able to ride out of this place and make a better life for yourselves." King tossed the bag onto the table, landing with a lucrative *thunk*. "We'll go over to the bank to settle up the rest."

"Assuming they have enough left," Frank said.

"If'n they don't, I'll see to it that you get a promissory note from the Governor."

Maribel tested the bag's weight, opened, and poured out a small waterfall of Western-world cousins to gold doubloons.

"We can get a coffin for Juan, a proper burial," Frank said.

"With enough left over to get us ahead on the restaurant," Maribel said. Looking up from the coin, she asked, "So, where you headed next?"

Leah watched King as the team leader formulated their extraction plan. She still had a zillion questions about how everything worked, and couldn't wait until they were on their own so she could break cover and get some answers.

"We'll head on to the next town that needs us. Don't like to stick around and put down roots. Doesn't sit well with me."

"King here gets antsy if he sleeps in the same bed twice," Roman said. "That's why we always trade out bedrolls."

Shirin winked at her teammate. "It's actually because Roman flattens them like an iron."

King excused himself to the facilities, and they sat and drank and talked for a good while longer before he came back and pulled the team upstairs.

King reported that HQ had given the all-clear on the patch, the breach and ripple effects over. He debriefed the team in a room of their own while Maribel and Frank made funeral arrangements for Juan.

The High Council had called the team back immediately, but King had convinced them the patch would be stronger if they stayed for the funeral.

So that afternoon, the Genrenauts stood in their finest, un-blood-stained clothes with Maribel and Frank as the local priest held a service for Juan Louis Mendoza. The Genrenauts helped lower the casket, then watched as Maribel and Frank let a handful of dirt pass through their hands as they said goodbye to their brother.

Leah stepped outside the moment, thinking about the shape of the story—beginning, middle, and end. Which brought them here, burying the dead alongside Mallery's fallen posse.

Once the caskets had been lowered to their final rest, the townsfolk lined up to thank Maribel.

The whole town.

Maribel had a receiving line four dozen folk long. Merchants, ranchers, the schoolmarm, the blacksmith, the two bankers left, and more.

The team stood by as the town embraced Maribel and Frank as their own. Some folks came over to thank them as well, but King waved them off, saying, "Maribel's the hero. We were just glad to help."

Leah watched the townsfolk with Maribel and her brother. "They're not going anywhere, are they?"

"Doubt it," King said, arm bound in a sling under his duster, one sleeve hanging empty.

When the townsfolk had said their piece, Maribel and Frank came to see the Genrenauts. Maribel's vest sported a shiny new tin star.

"So I reckon you're staying, then," King said.

"When an entire town begs you to stay, you consider."

Frank added, "And they offered to build my restaurant for me. Right there on the rail line. Folks will come from either coast."

Maribel looked back to the graves. "I just wish Juan could have lived to see it."

"We're going to call it Juan's Café," Frank said, squeezing his sister's hand.

"I think that's a fine way to honor him," King said. "It might be a long time before we make it back here. You look after this town now, you hear? I'll make sure the Governor gets a full report so you're not left on your own the next time trouble comes around."

Maribel settled into a wider stance, already embracing her role, like she took up more of the screen. "You got it. And make sure you look after each other too," Maribel said.

Roman and Shirin tipped their hats. Leah followed suit, and the four of them turned to walk off into the sunset, the cherry on top of the genre cake.

Mission Accomplished.

When the town was out of sight, the team turned and headed back to their ship.

Along the way, Leah unloaded her backlog of questions.

"So, what will happen to them now? If their story is done, do they disappear? If the whole world is supposed to be Western stories, what happens when your story is over?"

"They keep going on. The people here have real lives, but everyone is always in the beginning, middle, or end of a story. They get their happily-ever-afters, too," Shirin said.

"We only ever see people in the middle," King added. "When things run smooth, our presence actually disturbs the world more than it helps."

Roman said, "And regs dictate that we can't stay in the field for longer than a week unless absolutely necessary."

Cresting a hill, they returned to the rock outcropping that disguised the ship. The illusory stone was a shade off from the ones around it. Or maybe that was her nascent genre-senses tipping her off. Another one for the question bucket.

"Why a week?"

"Stay on a world too long, and the place gets its hooks in you," Roman said. "You start to get boxed in by the story—"

"That's enough about that," King said, cutting him off. The team leader had a remote-looking device in black plastic and pushed a button. The Phase Manipulator image fizzled out of existence, revealing the dust-coated rocket ship.

And the rest of the team's disguises dropped at the same time. Leah looked down and saw her own skin again, saw Shirin and King back to their real appearances. She felt like she'd exhaled a breath she hadn't known she'd been holding. She flexed her fingers and ran a hand over her arm.

"There'll be time for a proper debrief when we're back in HQ. Shirin, get our preflight going. Roman, the walk-around, and take the newbie with you."

Roman and Leah broke off and took a wide arc around the hill to approach the ship at ninety degrees to everyone else.

The Afrikaaner slipped back into teacher mode. "We go wide in case someone's been camping on the ship. We have proximity alarms, but even those can be disabled. Coming up on the ship, one, preferably two, members of the team do a visual inspection of the ship, looking for any holes in the fuselage, loose bolting, anything that seems out of order."

"Like a commercial flight, then?" Leah said, remembering the safety videos from the last time she'd gone home to visit her family. As far as she could tell, the ship looked fine, for an inter-dimensional snub-nosed rocketship. Still, anything that could keep them from having to deal with that amount of turbulence on the way back was worth a thorough check.

Roman ran his hands over the hull of the ship, feeling the seams. He sidestepped his way around the ship, tracking the base of the ship's trunk, where the tripod fin-legs splayed out from the body. "Any flight, really. Unless the pilot's lazy. And of course, when we have to get off-world in a hurry, that walk-around gets pretty cursory."

"And how often do you have to jet out like that?"

Roman opened a panel below the hatch and booted up a green-scale screen. "More often than I'd like, but not as often as you'd think. King's team has the highest completion rate in the organization. He's thorough, and he gets first pick of prospective recruits."

"How old is this ship?" Leah asked, pointing to the aged display.

"This one's fifteen years old. Most ships serve for about twenty years before they're retired. It's a Mark III. The Mark IVs are just now going into service at the Hong Kong and Mumbai bases."

"And where do we get all of this tech?" she asked.

Roman responded with a thin smile. "We, eh?"

"Hey, I risked life and limb, I think I've earned a we."

"So do I." Roman tapped at the console, the screen scrolling through dozens of lines of text. "Most of the tech comes from subsidiaries owned by the High Council. The workers don't know what they're making, everything is subdivided out, double-blind, then assembled at each base."

"Sounds absolutely Soviet."

"It's the best way to keep everyone safe. What we do is bigger than countries, bigger than economics, it's a literal world-saving kind of mission. But it's easiest if almost no one knows about it and they go about their lives happily oblivious. The blowback we'd get if the truth got out . . ." Roman shook his head.

"I can imagine Badger News going to town with something like this."

"Most people wouldn't even be able to appreciate the stakes, and even if they could, we'd immediately see people trying to travel between worlds for kicks, and others blaming every little social ill on some screw-up by a Genrenaut team."

Leah could just imagine what some politicians might do with the truth, let alone religious zealots. You'd see whole religions pop up or metamorphose into something new and probably even more bizarre. "Got it. Sacred burden, sworn to secrecy, all that jazz."

"Hey, the pay's good," Roman said. "Worth not being able to tell anyone I date what I really do."

"What do you tell them?"

"I work in a lab."

"That King's go-to?"

"It is. Ninety-nine percent of folks don't know enough science to poke a hole in the cover, and those that do, we distract with theoretical quantum physics and doctoral lit crit from King. It's not even really a lie. We're using a different version of the many worlds theory."

"Positing a relationship between parallel dimensions instead of individual emergence and digression, I guess." Her physics class had been at 2 p.m. Much better.

"Right in one. I was never much for science. You'll want to go to Shirin or King for the detailed breakdown. Or buy Preeti a drink and let her go to town. She's got a doctorate in Dimensional Theory."

"I disbelieve that that is a real thing in which one can get a degree."

"Officially, no. But the High Council funds a special

shadow department at top universities around the world. It's where they recruit most of their tech and science staff."

"I am officially down the rabbit hole, aren't I?"

"Pretty much. But you've handled yourself pretty well. Last newbie we had lost his lunch two hours into the first mission."

"Was that you?" Leah asked.

Roman shut the panel. "No, but I didn't fare much better. That was Tommy Suarez."

Wash out of the Genrenauts, get an HBO special. Not a bad retirement plan.

Roman looked the ship up and down, then said, "We're good. Let's go home."

Epilogue

Sign on the Dotted Line

THE TRIP BACK from Western world was far smoother than the way over. There was some chop as they crossed back through the rainbows-on-black sky of the space between dimensions, but on the shake-o-meter, it registered as Bumpy rather than Vomit-Cannon.

As Leah stepped out of the ship and onto the stairs built into the hatch, a support team of ten techs greeted the team. The techs converged on the ship like flies on a corpse. Science flies.

"How's Mallery?" King asked as soon as he touched down.

One of the techs said, "She's out of surgery and recovering. I'll let the nurses know to expect you. Council will want your report first."

"I imagine they'll understand if I check in with medical first," King said, waving the bandaged arm. "How did Louis's team fare?"

Leah tried to squirrel these details away, loose puzzle

pieces to be assembled later, when she knew more about this brilliant and mad place.

"Last report said that they were on level twenty of the tower, under heavy fire."

"Something is definitely going on," Shirin said, the last out of the ship.

"I'll report to the Council once medical has cleared me, you three head over to see Mallery. I want familiar faces greeting her when she wakes up, let her know we finished the job."

"Come on, Kid," Roman said. "It's only fair to show you what happens when things don't go as smoothly as they did for us."

"That was smooth?" Leah asked.

———

Roman double-timed it toward the medical wing. Leah had to jog to keep up with Shirin, who was only a couple of inches taller and yet managed to power walk almost as fast as Roman. The doctors had taken King off to another room, away from recovery.

The trio was greeted by a middle-aged nurse—a black woman who looked like she'd been up for twenty or so hours, wearing blue scrubs and bright pink Crocs.

"She's awake, but only one of you should go in at a

time. Don't let her move. She lost a lot of blood."

"Thank you, Ms. Rachelle," Roman said, moving immediately to the door.

"I guess he's going first," Leah said.

Rachelle said, "He's usually the one with the gunshot wounds. This is a nice change of pace." She turned on one foot and returned to her station, filled with file folders and a pair of flat-panel screens. How often did the Genrenauts get hurt that they needed their own medical facility? Though with the focus on secrecy Roman had indicated, it made sense to make their HQ its own contained facility, a one-stop world-saving shop.

Shirin put a hand on Leah's shoulder. "While we're here, let me take you on the tour and show you what we're up against. Roman will come get us when he's done."

"I assume they're close, then?" Leah asked, treading right over the matter of propriety.

"She's like a little sister to him."

"This is one of those 'team-is-like-your-family' things, isn't it?"

"Right in one." Shirin walked over to the next room. She double-checked the chart and said, "This is Eve. She caught a poisoned arrow running from an enraged tribe defending its sacred artifact in the Pulp world."

"Will she be okay?"

"We hope so. The poison isn't known on Earth Prime, but we think she's past the worst of it."

"Yikes. How many teams are there, here?"

Shirin continued down the hall "We've got thirteen Genrenauts on staff at this base, enough to form three teams if we all have to mobilize at once. But right now, we're down three agents. The third is Perry here—he lost a duel with the Baron of Farthingmunster, trying to defend the honor of the Lady Whipton."

"Regency world?" Leah hazarded. Shirin nodded.

"This job doesn't usually have this high a casualty rate, right?" Leah asked. "You mentioned that something is off."

"That's why King has to report right away. The disturbances on the story worlds have gotten bigger, like a dimensional monsoon season. And when we try to put things back on track, the worlds fight back, harder. I've never seen anything like it. The Council is taking a measured stance, not officially acknowledging that anything is wrong, but King is worried. That's why he went ahead and brought you in. We're getting short-staffed, having trouble keeping up with all of the disturbances."

"Sounds like an awesome time to start the job."

Shirin crossed her arms. "Come on. You're telling me you'd rather go back to working reception?"

"Hey, the only danger there is dying of boredom."

"Uh-huh. We'll see about that. In the meantime, let's head to the break room. I could use some coffee that doesn't taste like it was brewed with molasses."

———

After all the fuss about reporting immediately, King ended up standing at attention for twenty minutes in the broadcasting room, waiting for the High Council to call in.

The bullet had gone straight through the meat of his arm. He'd be shooting lefty for a while, but Dr. Douglas said it wouldn't take too long to heal, especially if they deployed on story-worlds like Action or Science Fiction that had rapid recovery.

King stood at the focal point between the three wide-screen flat-panel monitors that filled one wall of the room. Behind him and on both sides were the servers, processors, and transmission equipment to live-cast at three angles at high-fidelity across the world, while never being able to tell him where exactly his superiors were speaking to him from. He guessed they were based in Europe, but he'd always met the Councilors here, at his base, or at European HQ outside of London. But the London team was as in the dark as he was about where the Councilors really lived.

It'd been like that the whole thirty years he'd been with the organization, one of the first Genrenauts recruited by the Council during their initial expansion.

The screens changed from flat black to the loading screens, showing the array of dozens of worlds in their orbits around Earth, each marked by its official symbol. Pistols, hearts, fans, swords, magnifying lens, prayer beads, and so on. His team's beat was a small selection of the dozens of story worlds the Genrenauts patrolled and protected.

The title screen dropped, revealing five shadowed figures. They always stood in shadow, seeing King but never being seen during meetings. It'd been the same five of them, as near as he could tell, the entire thirty years. He'd only ever met three of the High Council. The other two, the most senior, never made public appearances. King had taken it as the eccentricity of the rich, germophobia, or something. They were a constant—inaccessible, unbending, but just.

The Council's leader, Gisler, spoke from the middle of the screen. "Angstrom King. Report."

"The breach has been patched, Councilor."

King unpacked the mission in exhaustive detail, relating Mallery's initial patch attempt, the complication, and his team's response, down to Leah's impressive first outing and the resolution, solidifying Maribel Mendoza as a hero and securing the town.

Fifteen minutes later, he was done.

"What is your agent's status?" another councilor asked.

"Mallery York is in serious but stable condition. She's the third operative from this base to be critically injured in the last month. I'm concerned about the nature of these recent breaches—"

D'Arienzo, friendliest of the Council, cut King off. "We are aware of your concerns, and the reports from team leaders about these so-called aberrations in the breaches. Our science division is investigating the readings, but thus far, we have no reason to believe that this is anything other than a seasonal high tide of dimensional disturbances—"

"With all due respect, Councilor—"

Gisler cut him off. "Respect means not interrupting your superiors."

Status. Respect. Propriety. His own team called him a stick in the mud, but if they only knew the Council . . .

D'Arienzo continued. "We thank you for your efforts, and for your report. Debrief your team and stand down to ready status."

"Understood," King said. And with that, the call dropped, the screens going blank.

"Pricks," King said under his breath once he was certain nothing would pick up his back talk.

Which was outside the room and ten paces down the hallway.

But that was the way of things. The Council were mysterious and aloof. But without them, none of this would be possible. They'd discovered dimensional breaches and travel between the worlds, and kept their eyes on the big picture, maintaining the delicate balance between dozens of worlds. They had earned the right to dictate terms.

———————

Two coffees in, Leah watched King walk into the break room and make himself some tea.

"So, what do you think of this operation?" he asked.

"You're all kind of suicidal. But I love it. There's no way even being a professional comedian could be this cool. Sure, it'd be less dangerous, but . . . cowboys, and lasers, and spaceships!"

"And that's probably all in your next two pay periods," Shirin said from the couch. Boots off and legs up, she had her nose in a thick tome of a biography.

"With Mallery injured, my team's understaffed for the foreseeable future. So, if you want it, there's a probationary position here for you. Your start would be back-dated to yesterday when you walked in the building."

"Isn't there some security screening I have to do?"

"I did all of that already. So, do you want the job?"

Leah was expecting the offer, since she'd manage to pull off the fight with her slapdash plan, but seeing the Genrenauts in traction had given her some pause. She could walk away right then and if King delivered, she'd have the solid gig, she could build her career and put this all behind her.

She thought back to the team at the table, to the look in Maribel's eyes as Matt Williamson dropped to the floor. She thought about Frank's cooking, Shirin's laugh, and the feeling of jet thrusters beneath her.

Red-pill, blue-pill time. She could go home, keep filing other people's paperwork while daydreaming material for her shows, or go down the rabbit hole into a totally bizarre and dangerous but exciting line of work hacking dimensions and saving the world with stories.

Mom and Dad would say to stay with the familiar, to dig deep and commit to her comedy that she had chosen over her family. But she'd gotten into comedy because it was the best way she knew to make a difference, to tell the stories she wanted to hear. In the Genrenauts, she could do all of that and never have to take minutes during a Strategic Revenue Best Practices presentation again.

"Can I Sandberg for a moment and ask about the pay

and benefits?" She'd never argued a salary before, but she'd gone into a firefight for this job. A little negotiation wasn't going to cost her the gig.

King pulled a slip of yellow legal paper out of his jacket and passed it to Leah.

She unfolded the paper and was disgusted at the low-ball figure until she realized there was an extra zero at the end.

"That first number is salary. In dollars. U.S. dollars?"

King said, "That it is. And below that is the health package."

Leah scanned the bottom half of the paper. The plan was positively *European*. Including a *lot* of life insurance. Unsurprising, but not super-reassuring.

"This job will call for long hours more often than any of us like, but I think you'll agree that the compensation is worth the overtime."

So, to review, she could stick with her mind-numbing but safe job and bang her head against the stand-up circuit with one gig a week until she refined her act enough to earn more work, or take a ridiculous-percent pay increase to do six impossible things before breakfast.

"You've got yourself a deal," Leah said, extending a hand. King's grip was unsurprisingly strong.

"Welcome to the team, then, Probie."

Really? "Why Probie? This isn't *NCIS*."

"The show didn't make that up. Fire departments and other agencies use it. And so do we."

"But this place isn't government, right?"

"No," King said. "We're technically nonstate actors, and if most governments found out about us, we'd probably be locked away forever. So read the NDA very, very closely."

"How's Mallery?" Leah asked, eager to change the subject from how much of a newbie she was and the hazing she should expect.

"She'll be fine," Roman said. "No major arteries hit, and she's already restless. Ms. Rachelle had to come in and up her sedative so she won't tear her stitches."

Roman offered a hand to Leah. "Welcome to the Genrenauts."

They shook. "Hope you survive the experience," he added.

His cribbing of the famous X-Men line put Leah even more at ease. She already felt at home with the troupe, this band of storytellers and hustlers. And she couldn't wait to tell off Suzanne at the office and move her army of office animals out of the cubicle and into the Genrenauts break room.

"Sounds good. But for now, I'm going to go and crash."

"Not so fast," King said. "Just because you've been

cleared, doesn't mean you get to skip the rest of the paperwork."

The team lead handed her a pen and a manila folder that was at least three inches thick. "I'll need these on my desk within the hour. Then you can head home. And be back tomorrow by eight for orientation."

"I take it back. I'll die of boredom. Anything to avoid paperwork." Leah hung her head as she exaggeratedly padded to a table, dropping the manila folder to as much despondent effect as she could muster.

A minute later, Roman sat down across from her, a tablet and earphones in one hand, a pair of bottled beers in the other. He twisted off the caps with his palm (nice trick), and passed one to Leah.

They toasted, and Roman put in his earbuds. He opened a digital comics reader on his tablet, leaving Leah to the stack. Leah repeated the ridiculous salary to herself as she scanned the stack of papers.

Camaraderie, adventures in storytelling, a fat paycheck, and health insurance. What more could a girl ask for?

END EPISODE ONE

Next time on Genrenauts . . .

Leah dives headlong into learning the skills of a Genre-naut—from PowerPoint presentations on narrative fore-casting to a rigorous course of readings and primary sources for genre awareness.

And oh, so much paperwork.

When a breach emerges in the Science Fiction world, the team takes flight for the cosmically cosmopolitan Ahura-3 station. Leah is thrown straight into the deep end of the station, filled with bumpy-headed aliens, galactic alliances, and space-faring mercenaries.

All of this and more in:

GENRENAUTS EPISODE 2:
THE ABSCONDED AMBASSADOR

Acknowledgments

I don't remember a time when I wasn't enthralled by storytelling. But it quickly grew into more than that—I came to be interested in the types of stories, the expectations they set, their shared vocabulary of characters and plots.

In other words: *genre*.

The first film that I remember watching that specifically invoked the idea of narrative genres and the rules that came with them was *The Last Action Hero*. But it was far from the last tale to hit me right in my story-fixation. Eventually, I was so caught up by stories that I designed a major to learn more about them. But that was just another beginning. I figure I'll be working through and from my fixation with stories and genre for as long as I can continue to write.

Genrenauts started as a toss-off joke about a woman from our world thrown into a stereotypical high fantasy realm, where she instantly pegs the goatee-wearing advisor as the bad guy because the goatee-wearing advisor is pretty much *always* the bad guy. That loving playfulness with genre expectations, archetypes, and time-honored tropes grew into a word: Genrenauts—people who travel to similarly rigid worlds. But why? And that, friends, was a question worth answering.

To build this idea into something capable of sustaining what is currently planned as a five-season arc, I did what I normally do—I piled on influences like they were mix-ins at a boutique ice cream shop, taking familiar flavors and combining them with my own perspective and sense of humor.

I believe in citing your sources, and specifically inspired by Austin Kleon's *Steal Like an Artist*, I'm making good on that.

The conceptual bones of Genrenauts are informed by: *Quantum Leap, Leverage, The Librarians, Planetary, Sliders, Indexing, The Last Action Hero, Redshirts, Primetime Adventures,* a fistful of Choose Your Own Adventure novels, and probably several other touchstones I'm not even consciously aware of. In terms of the episodic format, I was influenced by TV shows like *Babylon 5, Leverage,* and *The Librarians* again, as well as the idea of fiction-as-serial-TV projects like *The Beam* or *Yesterday's Gone*.

And as Genrenauts has many influences, I had just as many helpers along the way to this first installment in the series.

First, my ceaseless thanks to Meg White—my first reader, confidant, brainstorming buddy, and so much more.

Big high-fives to Megan Christopher and Ron Mitchell for the initial gut check.

Huge props to Dave Robison for brainstorming awesomeness, encouraging me to dig deeper with the central concept.

Massive thanks to Beth Cato, Effie Seiberg, Kate Walton, and Daniel Bensen for their invaluable feedback and support.

A hearty round of applause to Patrick S Tomlinson for his insights into the world of stand-up comedy.

Emphatic head-nods of gratitude to fellow Tor.com novella series author Matt Wallace for his support and encouragement as we take the literary world by storm with novella magic.

Three cheers for my fellow *Skiffy and Fanty Show* peeps for the exciting and stimulating discussions of media and storytelling, keeping my genre senses sharp.

Continued thanks to my agent, Sara Megibow, for following my flight of fancy and selling the series.

A toast of thanks to my former colleague and now editor Lee Harris, for believing in the series and bringing me into the Tor.com family.

Thank you to Irene Gallo and Peter Lutjen for briefing and designing a wonderful cover to set the tone for the series look.

To Mordicai Knode I award 1000 XP of gratitude for

his help in spreading the word.

Last, but not least, my undying thanks to you, the reader. Whether this is our first dance together or if you've been with me since *Geekomancy*, thank you for your support and your part in bringing this story to life.

About the Author

Photograph © Brandie Roberts

MICHAEL R. UNDERWOOD has circumnavigated the globe, danced the tango with legends, and knows why Tybalt cancels out Capo Ferro. He also rolls a mean d20.

He is the author of the Ree Reyes urban fantasies, fantasy superhero novel *Shield and Crocus,* supernatural thriller *The Younger Gods,* and Genrenauts, a comedic science fiction novella series. By day, he's the North American Sales & Marketing Manager for Angry Robot Books.

Mike lives in Baltimore with his fiancée and their ever-growing library. In his rapidly vanishing free time, he makes pizzas from scratch and reads comics by the pound. He is a cohost on the Hugo-nominated *Skiffy and Fanty Show.*

TOR·COM

Science fiction. Fantasy.
The universe.
And related subjects.

*

More than just a publisher's website, Tor.com is a venue for **original fiction, comics,** and **discussion** of the entire field of SF and fantasy, in all media and from all sources. Visit our site today — and join the conversation yourself.

CPSIA information can be obtained at www.ICGtesting.com
Printed in the USA
LVOW11s1401131115

462465LV00003B/35/P